Images

Heartlines

Books by Pam Lyons
A Boy Called Simon
He Was Bad
It Could Never Be . . .
Latchkey Girl
Danny's Girl

Books by Anita Eires
Tug Of Love
Summer Awakening
Spanish Exchange
Star Dreamer
Californian Summer
If Only . . .
Teacher's Pet

Books by Mary Hooper
Love Emma XXX
Follow That Dream
My Cousin Angie
Happy Ever After

Books by Barbara Jacobs
Two Times Two

Books by Jane Pitt
Loretta Rose
Autumn Always Comes

Books by Ann de Gale
Island Encounter

Books by Anthea Cohen
Dangerous Love

Books by Silwyn Williams
Give Me Back My Pride

Books by Ann Ruffell
Friends For Keeps

Books by Lorna Read
Images

Heartlines

Lorna Read

Images

A Pan Original

First published 1985 by Pan Books Ltd,
Cavaye Place, London SW10 9PG
9 8 7 6 5 4 3 2 1
© Lorna Read 1985
ISBN 0 330 287060
Printed and bound in Great Britain by
Hunt Barnard Printing, Aylesbury, Bucks
This book is sold subject to the conditions that it
shall not, by way of trade or otherwise, be lent, re-sold,
hired out, or otherwise circulated without the publisher's prior
consent in any form of binding or cover other than that in which
it is published and without a similar condition including this
condition being imposed on the subsequent purchaser

Chapter 1

'Griff won't keep you a minute.' The blonde girl at the reception desk gave me a friendly smile. 'He's on a call to Los Angeles, so if you'd like to take a seat over there...'

She indicated a long, beige leather couch which was over against the wall, and I sat down, frowning slightly to myself. I'd spotted the advertisement for a 'Junior Girl Friday for six weeks only' in one of the free magazines that I'd picked up at the tube station. I had no idea what kind of firm it was. When I'd rung up to enquire about the job, the girl who'd made the appointment for me had just answered the phone with the words: 'G.R. Agency,' leaving me none the wiser.

I'd expected it to be some kind of temp agency, but this reception area was straight out of a sophisticated television series. It wasn't a bit like the grotty old offices my dad works in, with their brown paint that looks as if it's been there since the time of Queen Victoria, and their rat-gnawed skirting boards. (Or maybe it's only mice, but very big ones.) No, in this place your feet sank up to the ankles in soft beige tufts, and the walls were a fresh, subtle honey shade. There was a long brass-and-glass coffee table in front of me with a pile of magazines on it. The top one was something called *Music Week*.

When I spotted it, I felt a jolt of excitement. Surely this place wasn't connected with the music business? That would be too good to be true. I hadn't been a bit nervous up till now, because I hadn't cared one way or another about the job, figuring it was highly unlikely I'd get it, but now I was really interested. I'm not the sort of girl who spends all my pocket money on records and concert tickets, but I do like certain singers and groups, and always try to watch the pop programmes on television, to keep up with what's happening, especially the latest fashions. They interest me almost more than the music.

The receptionist pulled a lever on the switchboard in front of her, then swung round in her swivel chair and stood up. She was wearing an extremely short Sixties-style mini-dress, white, with bright orange swirls on it, and she had matching orange tights and white shoes. I approved.

'Can I get you a coffee while you're waiting, Belinda?' she enquired. 'I think Griff's going to be on this call for some time.'

I liked the way everyone seemed to be on first-name terms with everybody else, even the boss. It seemed as if you could wear whatever you wanted, too. As soon as the girl had gone out to fetch my coffee, I whipped out my handbag mirror and gave myself the once-over.

'You're never going to an interview dressed like *that*!' Mum had challenged me this morning. 'No one'll give you a job if you go there looking such a . . . such a . . .'

'Freak?' I'd supplied politely, but I was seething

inside. There was nothing wrong with the way I dressed. My clothes didn't leave any bits of me exposed which should have been covered. They weren't an eyesore. The colours were very tastefully chosen – by me. I loved designing and making my own things. For the last year or so, I'd been going through what I liked to think of as my 'medieval revival' period. Whilst browsing through the public library, mugging up for my O-level History paper, I'd come across a really interesting book illustrating the fashions they wore in those days. Hats, shoes and even undergarments were pictured in minute detail, and the rich materials, the tapestries and velvets, slashed, appliquéd, padded and laced, had me filling my notepad with sketches instead of dates of battles.

Today, I was wearing an outfit I always felt really relaxed and happy in – wine-coloured tights, flat burgundy patent shoes, and a short tunic dress made out of a soft purple material, padded at the shoulders and laced round the waist and up the bodice with gold cord. I'd put my hair in heated rollers before coming out, so it hung down my back in chestnut ringlets, held back from my face with two small gold slides.

Apart from a touch of greyish-pink eyeshadow in the hollows of my cheekbones, to accentuate them, and a smudge of very pale gold colour on my eyelids, I wore no make-up. I hated lipstick anyway. Whenever I wore it, it always got smudged, whereas other people's seemed to stay immaculate all day. I wish I knew their secret.

'Here we are. I say, where did you get your dress from? It's most unusual.' The return of the receptionist made me jump, as the carpet had muffled her footsteps and I hadn't heard her. Hoping she hadn't caught me examining my reflection, because I didn't want her thinking I was some vain little poser, I palmed my mirror swiftly back into my bag and accepted the steaming mug of coffee she was offering me.

'I – well, actually, I made it,' I confessed, sipping at the scalding liquid. She muttered something complimentary, and returned to her swivel chair, on which she could swing easily from her typewriter to the switchboard. I wondered how on earth she managed to do two jobs at once.

As she dealt with some incoming calls, I tried to combat my nerves by taking deep breaths and trying to think of something else – anything but the fact that I was awaiting an interview for a holiday job. I prayed that there wouldn't be many people after it, as it was only for six weeks, then realised how many other schoolkids like me were frantically seeking a few weeks' work. Please, *please* . . . I prayed, crossing my fingers tightly. Of course I want everybody at every school to get a job. I'm not completely selfish. But please let me get this one . . .

There was a beeping sound on the switchboard, and the girl called to me. 'Griff will see you now. His office is down there, second door on the right. Just leave your cup on the table, I'll see to it. Good luck.'

I went off down the corridor, thinking glumly that she probably said that to every interviewee. Walking towards that door felt like wading against an incoming tide, the waves I was forcing myself against being those of my own crippling terror.

The door was already open. The first thing I saw, on the opposite wall of the room, were three framed gold discs. So it *was* a music company! I thought exultantly. Then my gaze flicked to the desk. It was new and shiny, and a pair of large feet in blue and yellow trainers were propped up on it. My eyes carried on from them to their owner. Surely he couldn't be the boss? I thought. He was far too young. His fuzzy hair stood out in a halo round his head, which was resting on his arms which were folded behind it.

'Hello,' he greeted me casually. 'Which one are you?'

My instant reaction was: how rude! 'Belinda Harker,' I told him. This wasn't at all what I'd expected. I'd read articles on how to conduct job interviews, and this was nothing like any of them. I was completely puzzled.

He yawned widely, and I thought how ill-mannered and off-hand he was. He waved a weary hand towards a chair and asked me to sit down.

'How old are you?' was his next question. At least he'd taken his feet off the table now.

'Seventeen in September,' I replied, my voice coming out louder than I'd intended. Now it was me who sounded rude. 'Didn't I say so in my letter?' I added.

'Aha . . . Virgo or Libra. What date?' he shot at me.

I couldn't get over what a weirdo he was. But at least he was interesting, and I began to warm to him. I sometimes read my horoscope in the paper, but I'd never really taken astrology seriously. This bloke obviously did.

'I'm a Libra – September 23rd,' I informed him.

'That's good,' he replied. 'We should get on. I'm a

Gemini. Now, let me see. You said in your letter that you were still at school and hoping to do some A-levels and get into art college,' he said, glancing at a piece of paper which I recognised as the letter I'd sent after being requested to by the girl who had taken my original phone call. I'd stewed for hours over that letter, wondering whether to make it chatty or extremely formal, and ending up with a mixture of the two.

'That's right,' I told him.

'I suppose I've really got to ask you all these boring questions,' he remarked, stretching and yawning again. 'Sorry about this. Only got back from the States yesterday. One of our bands...' He broke off abruptly as my eyes widened, then he went on, 'We didn't mention what we did in our ad because we didn't want to attract the wrong sort of people. The last thing we wanted was to be inundated with would-be groupies who haven't any intention of working but just want to hang around the musicians,' he explained.

I leaned forward in my chair and felt sure my interest was written all over my face.

'G.R. stands for me – Griff Roberts. Welsh, you know, look you?' I grinned as he put on an exaggerated Welsh accent. 'We're a management agency, handle bands and some solo artistes, arrange bookings, look after them on the road. I've got a partner, Joe Turner. He's not in yet. Late night, up till three at a club, listening to a new band we're thinking of taking on. You can't keep regular hours in this sort of business. We all end up killing ourselves.'

'Then why do you do it?' I asked, and suddenly bit

my lip in horror, marvelling at my cheek. I'd been talking to him just as if he were . . . well, a friend, someone of my own age. Yet I should have been treating him like a prospective boss. I'll never get the job now, I thought, mentally kicking myself for being so stupid.

He thought for a moment, as if I really had asked him an intelligent question. Then he smiled, a sudden beam, showing rather crooked teeth. 'Dunno. Because I wasn't good enough to be in a band myself, I suppose!'

The articles I'd read about how to conduct yourself at interviews had all advised the interviewee to ask questions. If you sat there and said nothing, your interviewer would either think you too shy, too stupid, or not very keen. So I plunged in. 'What exactly would my job consist of?'

'Your letter says you can type a bit.' He stared at me with cool blue eyes.

'Yes, we've done some in school. I'm not brilliant, more like sixty minutes a word than sixty words a minute!' I joked. It was a gag I'd often used, but, too late, I realised this was totally the wrong time and place. Strangely, all my nerves seemed to have gone. This guy's casualness had put me at my ease.

'Then you'd be helping Sarah out — she's the bird on the switchboard, and she doubles as our secretary at the moment. You'd be making a few phone calls, picking up airline tickets, that sort of thing. In fact, you'd be chief gofer.'

'Chief *what*?' I'd always thought a gopher was some kind of buck-toothed American rodent, a cross between a rabbit and a guinea-pig. Surely he didn't think I looked like one of those?

'Gofer. It's a music biz term and it means the person you tell to go for this, and go for that,' he explained.

'Oh, I see!' I said, and couldn't help laughing.

'You seem the only intelligent, switched-on person of all the girls I've seen,' he announced suddenly. His remark really threw me and I kept silent, not knowing how I should react. 'All these boring little chicks in their nice, neat little skirts and blouses, who sit there like mice and haven't got any style or originality,' he went on. 'That's what getting a hit record, or being a hit group, is all about. Image. Style. You've got it. I've never seen an outfit like that before in my life. Did you buy it in one of those theatrical costume sales?'

He didn't give me a chance to answer. As I sat there congratulating myself on not giving in to Mum this morning when she wanted me to wear something more ordinary, I heard his light, lazy voice inform me: 'The job's yours if you want it.'

Chapter 2

I don't remember leaving the office. I guess I must have floated out in a daze. Griff asked me if I could start the very next day, and of course I told him I could. I had been looking forward to a few days to myself. After all, school had only broken up last Friday and I'd been hoping to go round a few art galleries and take in the latest exhibitions. Then I reminded myself that, as I'd be working in the centre of London, I'd be able to do that sort of thing in my lunch hours. Any last, lingering regret at my sudden loss of freedom disappeared at the magic thought of working in the music business.

On the way back to the tube station, I suddenly realised that there wasn't much point in going straight home, as there'd be nobody in to tell my great news to. Dad was at work, and Mum worked in the mornings, typing for a local firm of solicitors. In the end, I decided to go and see my best mate, Karen. I knew she'd be jealous as anything when I told her. She had a Saturday job in a supermarket, which she'd been doing for ages. It was really tiring and boring, but she was hoping they'd be able to give her some extra days' work over the hols.

I rang her from the tube station and said I had something really important to tell her. I deliberately made my voice sound as mysterious as possible.

'Don't tell me,' she squawked down the receiver, 'you've met some guy in Soho who asked you to star in his latest movie, a touching, artistic saga of first love called "Schoolgirl in Suspenders." '

We both giggled. It was one of our 'in' jokes that we always said 'in suspenders' instead of 'in suspense'.

'In that case,' I said haughtily, 'I'm going to keep *you* in suspenders till I get there!'

As I sailed down the escalator, I felt sure there was a kind of shimmering glow all around me that marked me out as special, and a success. I noticed people staring at me, and felt I should give them a languid wave, like the Queen does. Then I calmed down and realised they were only staring at my clothes. People usually did.

'It's pretty well door-to-door for you on the tube, isn't it?' Griff had remarked. As I got off the tube at Ealing Broadway, I realised he was right. It had only taken about half an hour from Oxford Circus, too, so the daily journey wasn't going to be too bad.

To my surprise, when I got to Karen's house, it wasn't her who opened the door but her elder brother, Ian.

'Hi, Bin-bag,' he greeted me airily, with a kind of sarcastic twist to one corner of his mouth. Karen swore she'd caught him practising that expression in his bedroom mirror. He'd called me Bin-bag more or less ever since he'd met me, because he insisted it sounded like Belinda and suited me better. The rotten swine!

'Hi, Boring,' I chirped back. He didn't like me calling him that any more than I liked his nickname for me, but I'd told him several times that he deserved it on account of the straight, unimaginative clothes he always wore. He wasn't scruffy, but he was . . . well, kind of neutral, I suppose, usually to be found in head-to-toe shades of brown.

Personality-wise, though, I had to admit I found him far from boring. In fact, I wished he *had* been thick, or nasty, or even as neutral as his clothes, because then I'd never have to think about him. And I did — a lot.

'They didn't need your brain-cells in the office today, then?' I enquired. Ian had done brilliantly in his A-levels, but had thrown up the chance to go to university in order to start work in an advertising agency. 'From the bottom upwards,' he had informed me when he first started. 'I'll be helping think up ideas for a baby powder account!'

'It wasn't that,' he said now. 'My bed sprouted arms in the night and wouldn't let me go.'

I felt a sharp twinge of jealousy at the thought that perhaps he'd smuggled someone in with him, then I dismissed the idea. No, he was just joking, I told myself sternly. All the same, the word 'bed' in connection with Ian did very strange things to my insides.

I pushed past him to go in and see Karen, but he put an arm across the doorway and stopped me.

'Password!' he demanded.

'Er . . . weasels,' I suggested, saying the first weird word that popped into my head.

'That'll do,' he decided, and let me through. 'You're looking good today,' he remarked as I headed up the stairs towards Karen's den. I froze in my tracks. It was only about the second time ever that Ian had said anything nice to me, and I couldn't believe it. In fact, I could feel my face growing boiling hot and bright red. I wondered whether I ought to say anything, and then, in panic, decided it would be best to pretend I hadn't heard him, so I carried on up the stairs.

The IN/OUT sign on Karen's door was turned to IN, so I waltzed straight in without knocking. As I'd expected, she had her nose in a book. She looked up when I entered, and pushed her specs back up her nose. Then, miracle of miracles, she actually put her book down, having first marked her page with a scrap of paper. I glanced disapprovingly at her. She looked a real scruff-bag in a tatty old sweatshirt and her most battered jeans, but I had too much on my mind to start lecturing her.

She folded her arms. 'Well . . ?' she invited.

'I didn't expect to see Ian here,' I remarked, deliberately keeping her on the boil.

'Oh, he had to go to the dentist's first thing, so he's taken the morning off. Come on, Belinda, spill the beans!'

I crouched down, pushed aside the various books and magazines that littered Karen's bedroom floor, and made myself space to sit down on her bedside rug. Karen was absent-mindedly chewing a strand of her long hair. It was a disgusting, unhygienic habit which I'd told her off about often.

She saw that I'd noticed. 'If you don't tell me soon, I'll bite a chunk off and eat it!' she threatened. At the thought, the back of my throat went all crawly, as if I had a hair stuck in it.

Karen didn't even know I'd applied for the job. I'd decided to keep it a complete secret, even from her, although we normally shared every little thing, apart from my mixed-up feelings for her brother!

'I've got a job,' I announced proudly.

'What? Oh, that's great! Is it in a shop or something?' She was bouncing up and down on the edge of her bed with excitement, and there was a crash as a heap of papers slid off. 'Damn! There goes the research for the talk on locusts I'm going to give at the Youth Club,' she grumbled, pulling a face. Karen had some strange interests. Mind you, she *was* studying Zoology . . .

'You're speaking to a superstar now, my dear.' I placed a hand on my hip and leant nonchalantly back against her bookcase, but regretted it when the overloaded article started to sway, and rocked back into a upright position again.

'Don't tell me . . . they've taken you on at the record shop in the new precinct.' As if it had a will of its own, her right hand crept towards the book she had so recently closed in my honour, and I knew I'd better tell her the rest quickly, before she lost interest.

'I've got a job in a proper office in the West End. It'll last most of the holiday. And it's not a record shop, it's a record company. Well, sort of. They manage some of the top bands in London—'

'Which ones?' Karen put in sharply, as if trying to catch me out in a fanciful lie.

'I don't know yet. I'll find out tomorrow — that's when I'm starting. But Griff — he's the boss — is great. I haven't met his partner yet, but if he's anything like Griff . . .' I waggled my eyebrows suggestively and Karen screwed her face up.

'Why didn't you tell me you'd applied for it?' she accused, looking really upset. 'That's if you're not making it up . . .'

'Of course I'm not,' I said, feeling quite hurt. 'And I'll tell you why I didn't let you in on it. It was a sort of superstition. I felt that the fewer people who knew about it, the better. Anyway, I didn't even know they had anything to do with groups till I got there. It looked like any other boring old job from the advertisement . . .' I sighed heavily, guessing I was in for one of Karen's moodies.

'Lucky old you...' she said in hollow, envious, super-gloomy tones. 'I can't even get any extra work at the shop, not unless anyone leaves or something.'

I glanced at my watch and suddenly realised Mum would be back and dying to hear how I'd got on. I scrambled to my feet and one of my knees made an alarming cracking noise.

'Rheumatics!' commented Karen sarcastically.

'Look, I want to come round later with something I'm making,' I told her. She was about my height, though she was a bit bustier, but I'd got over being envious. I generally used her as a human dressmaker's dummy whenever I was working on anything.

'If you must...' she muttered, and all I saw was the light from her window striking off her specs, turning them into blinding, opaque discs as I went out of her room.

I knew it was my fault that my news had struck a sour note with Karen, but I couldn't help this silly superstition of mine. I'd had to tell my parents, of course, otherwise Mum would have wanted to know where I was going this morning and I would have had to make up some lie or other. Mind you, although I disapproved of lying, it would have saved me all the fuss about what to wear.

One thing I really liked about Mum was that she didn't make herself a slave to her family. She wasn't one of those women who moan if you're five minutes late for a meal. During the school holidays, she'd get some lunch for us both if I was in, and if not, she'd leave me to fend for myself, which I thought was very sensible of her.

When I got in, she was sitting at the table munching crispbread, cheese and celery. She greeted me with her mouth full, and giggled as she tried to ask: 'Any luck?'

I nodded. 'I thought you always had to wait ages to hear anything, but they're so desperate for someone that they've offered me the job straight away!'

Mum swallowed convulsively, and brushed some imaginary crumbs from her lipstick. 'That's lovely! I'm very pleased for you, love. Mind you . . .' She got that look in her eye which, I knew only too well, meant that an insult was on its way, '. . . they *must* be desperate if they want *you*!'

'Mum!' I shrieked in exasperation, then went over and hugged her. I adored both my parents. I felt really sorry for those schoolmates of mine who had unhappy home lives. I was very lucky in that department, even to the extent that, when I got to Mum's age, I knew I wouldn't mind looking like her. She was slim and, while she wasn't outrageous like me, she certainly knew how to put clothes together. She had fairish hair, though, while mine was like Dad's.

'Tell me all about it, then,' she invited. I sat down, poured myself a cup of tea and related the morning's adventures.

I spent the afternoon working on a jacket I was making and after tea, I headed once more for Karen's. To my surprise, the bookworm had emerged from its den and was playing records in the lounge with Ian and a couple of his mates. Ian actually smiled when he saw me come in.

'You ought to get well in with Bin-bag here,' he told his friends. 'She's going to be a millionairess clothes designer one of these days . . . salon in Paris and all that.'

'Huh! We know all about what goes on in Paris, don't we?' one of his slimy mates said, nudging Ian and giving me a suggestive leer. Trust someone to spoil everything, I thought grumpily, as Karen and I headed up the stairs to the whistled strains of the Marseillaise. I knew they were thinking of the rude words, rather than the proper ones.

'I'm sorry I was so snotty with you earlier on,' Karen apologised. 'I'm really pleased for you – honest! I can't deny that I'm jealous, though. Can't you get me a job there, too? I'm a great tea maker . . . ouch!'

One of the pins holding my latest creation together had scratched her as she was gingerly wriggling into it. Then her long hair got tangled up with the collar, or stuffed down the sleeve or something, and it was an awful struggle to release her. I couldn't help laughing as she stood there, red in the face and with her specs all skew-whiff. 'Just remember, it's all in the cause of furthering the course of British fashion design, making the country rich again, and all that,' I reminded her.

She sighed. 'You're going to be rich all right, with six weeks' wages in your pocket,' she sniffed.

A lurch of excitement made my stomach turn over. Tomorrow, I was starting my job. I knew I wouldn't sleep a wink . . .

Chapter 3

Trust my luck for there to be a signal failure so that my train was delayed nearly twenty minutes. I sat there, getting tenser and tenser, as more and more people crammed into the carriage, making the temperature rise to an unbearable stickiness which rendered all my efforts to start the day looking clean and fresh totally pointless. Some stupid man bashed my knee with his briefcase. Not only did it hurt, it snagged my tights, which were an unusual shade of blue which had taken me ages to track down. I glared at him, wishing that I were a witch and could send him an instant plague of warts, or something equally nasty.

Then somebody's baby started howling, in a shrill, ear-splitting tone which completely set my teeth on edge. I closed my eyes and tried to remember what I'd read about how to meditate, but nothing happened; I wasn't swept into another dimension, or brought face to face with a big blue Buddha. Then, thankfully, the train started and I heaved a great sigh of relief.

I was supposed to be there for nine-thirty, but it was a quarter to ten before I trotted breathlessly up the stairs. Sarah was already there. It may have been my imagination, but I got the impression that she wasn't altogether pleased with me for being late.

'I thought perhaps you'd changed your mind since yesterday,' she said, quite humorously, but with a slight edge to her tone. I suppose I could be accused of being hyper-sensitive, but I've always been quick to pick up on other people's true thoughts and feelings, the things that lie behind their facial expressions.

'I'll put you where Sandy usually sits,' she told me, and led me through the first door on the left down the corridor. I couldn't see the desk at first, it was so hidden by filing cabinets and cardboard boxes.

'We haven't been in these offices long,' she explained. 'One of your jobs will be to try and sort some of this lot out.'

'Er . . . what's happened to Sandy?' I asked hesitantly. The whole set-up in the office seemed so disorganised and strange that I was quite expecting to hear that she'd accompanied some band to one of the Arab countries and had been kidnapped by white-slavers.

'In hospital, poor thing, having her appendix out. It was very infected and there were complications, so the doctors say she must take six weeks off to recover,' Sarah told me, solemn-faced.

I shuddered. Going to the dentist was a bad enough ordeal for me, so I didn't want to imagine what it must be like having to have a part of your anatomy removed!

'Tell you what, before I give you anything to do, I'll take you round and introduce you to the others,' she suggested. 'Oh damn, there goes the switchboard.' She scurried out as a loud beeping noise echoed down the corridor, and I settled myself behind the desk, feeling very strange indeed. Following yesterday's success, I'd come out in another of my creations today, but I was disappointed to find Sarah was looking quite ordinary, in a pair of jeans and a white satiny blouse.

Sarah bustled back, and I leapt to my feet and followed her. 'We're quite a small bunch, and we're not very frightening!' she assured me cheerfully. 'I'll just explain the set-up before we go in,' she added, pausing outside a closed door. 'G.R. are just starting their own small record label, too, so we've taken on a guy who used to work for one of the major record companies, and knows all about it. That's Paul. Then we pay a freelance record plugger, Dez, who comes in and out. There's Chrissy – she does some PR for us—'

'What's PR?' I interrupted her.

'Public Relations. It means trying to get the bands mentioned in the press, and on radio and television. Sort of co-ordinating between the musicians and the public. Chrissy's self-employed – she does publicity for other groups besides ours – but she rents office space here and concentrates on our product.'

'So what does a record plugger do, then?' I asked, rather bewildered. This was a whole new world to me and I was fascinated, yet I felt a real dumbo because I knew so little about it. However, Sarah didn't seem to mind my asking. Indeed, she seemed pleased at the opportunity to show off her superior knowledge.

'A record plugger's the guy who all our fortunes rest on,' she said importantly. 'When you think that there's anything up to a hundred, sometimes even more, records released every week, you can't expect the radio dee-jays to sit and listen to them all. What they'll do is have a flip through, pick out the names they recognise and discard the rest. A new recording artist hardly stands a chance. However good the record, the dee-jay will simply put it to one side, unless it catches his attention because it's particularly gimmicky or something.

'What the plugger does is build up a good, friendly relationship with as many dee-jays as he can, then he'll take your brand new record by the unheard-of band in and say, "Come on, do us a great favour and play this one on your ten a.m. show." '

'What about this hyping you hear about in the papers every so often?' I asked.

'Well, we'd never descend to anything like that,' Sarah said sharply, as if I were accusing the G.R. Agency of skulduggery. Then her face softened. 'Sorry to be so much on the defensive,' she apologised. 'It's just that Joe, Griff's partner, got mixed up in some funny business a few years back. It wasn't his fault, it was his boss at the time who was the crook, but Joe's name got hauled into it. Apparently he was bribing everyone who could be bribed – people in the record shops where the charts are compiled, dee-jays, you name it. And ... I might as well tell you this—' Sarah's voice dropped to a near-whisper, '—I'm Joe's girlfriend. We live together. He got me the job here. I'm not a very good typist though, so Griff isn't altogether pleased about it, but at least I know how to handle the switchboard. And, as Griff says—' she shot a venomous look towards his door, '—I'm decorative enough to have in the front office. Ooh, I do hate male chauvinist pigs, don't you?' she asked emphatically.

'I certainly do. I've met a few, too.' I was thinking

about Ian's mates. Some of the blokes at school were beasts to girls, too. You'd think that, at sixteen or seventeen, they'd be old enough to know better, but Griff was about twenty-eight or so. Maybe some men never learned. Or perhaps it was all a pose, I reflected.

Sarah took me into Paul's office. He was a tiny, wiry guy whose hair was already receding at the front although he couldn't have been more than twenty-two. He was wearing jeans and a tee-shirt with AARDVARK written across it, which I assumed was the name of a band. He looked bright and boppy and I quite took to him, though I couldn't have fancied him.

Chrissy wasn't in yet, so I was taken off to meet Sarah's boyfriend, Joe. Immediately I clapped eyes on him, I thought how lucky she was. He was quite a bit older than Sarah – in his early thirties, I would have thought – but he was tall, slim, with dark brown hair and piercingly blue eyes, and his white jeans and tee-shirt accentuated his slight tan.

'Pleased to meet you,' he said charmingly, shaking my hand. 'I must say Griff was quite right – you are rather spectacular,' he added, taking in my knickerbocker outfit. But he didn't say it in a chauvinist pig way; rather, he was paying tribute to my clothes, and I grinned happily back, then hoped Sarah wouldn't take it wrong and get jealous.

To say Sarah gave me plenty of work to do that day was an understatement. I was told to start work on the mountain of boxes, putting press releases together with photographs and slipping them into envelopes, but by the end of the day I'd scarcely finished half. I was feeling quite depressed until Griff popped his head in at about four-thirty to see how I was doing and remarked, 'Great Scott!' Then he yelled down the corridor, 'Hey, Joe, come and see this. We've got Wonderwoman working here!'

Joe looked in and smiled approvingly, and then Griff warned, 'No need to wear yourself out, kid. We don't want your mum phoning us in tears and saying, "What have you done with my daughter in that wicked office of yours? She's got so thin, she just slipped down the plug-hole in the bath!" '

Griff was so zany that I just fell about laughing. I didn't care if he *was* a male chauvinist pig, he was cheerful and funny and I liked him.

At home that evening, I just couldn't stop myself talking about my first day at work. 'And you should have seen my face when Sarah asked me to type some envelopes and I found it was an electric typewriter,' I chuckled. 'I sat there for ages, without a clue as to what all the levers and keys were for. I couldn't even get the thing switched on! I had to go and ask Sarah in the end and even so, once I'd got it going, the damn thing ran away with me and typed about ninety-five full-stops!'

Dad had a slightly glazed look in his eye as he tried to concentrate on what the TV news announcer was saying, but Mum smiled understandingly. 'Oh, by the way, Karen phoned,' she told me. 'She wanted to know how you'd got on and I said you'd call her back. Don't be on too long though,' she warned. 'Your dad's been going on about the size of the last phone bill. I don't think he wants another one like it.'

I took her advice and told Karen I'd come round tomorrow night and tell her all about it. However, I thought I'd make her laugh by telling her about the typewriter incident, and I was just in the middle of my account when I heard her give a sharp intake of breath, then heard noises in the background.

'What's going on?' I asked her, a little crossly, because I'd thought my tale was riveting enough to keep her interested.

'It's Ian and his new girlfriend,' she told me all excitedly. 'He's only just met her and I've never seen her before. She's just called for him in her car . . .'

'*Her* car?' I put in sharply. 'Is she rich or something?'

'Hang on . . .' I heard the sound of the receiver being put down. Then, seconds later, it was picked up again. 'I've just been looking out of the window. I didn't see much of her, but she was terribly smartly dressed – the Country Casual look, if you know what I mean. Sloane Ranger and all that. Not a bit Ian's type. What were you saying, now?'

I continued my story, but the fun had gone out of me and my anecdote now sounded flat and boring. How *could* Ian go out with someone like that? I caught myself thinking. How dare he have a girlfriend at all? But I mustn't think like that, I reminded myself. I'd never seen myself as his girlfriend, now had I? Ian and I were just mates. He was just Karen's brother. He'd never ask out someone called *Bin-bag*, I thought bitterly. And I wouldn't want to go out with anyone who dressed as boringly as he did! I told myself firmly. He had no flair, no style, no image. He wasn't the sort of man for me. I could have drawn on paper the kind of guy I figured was right . . . tall, skinny, hollow-cheeked, full of nervous energy, fantastically creative, maybe a photographer or something, or even an artist. A man who wasn't afraid of colours, who'd wear emerald greens and royal purples and singing, stunning yellows.

Up in my bedroom, I reached for my sketchpad and began to draw. But the ideal man kept turning out to have Ian's face. Ian *was* tall and skinny and energetic. I could just picture him in a flowing, toga-like tunic over tight, tight trousers that fitted like a second skin. A cream tunic and a purple velvet cloak.

In frustration, I tore the drawings from my pad and crumpled them up. But Ian's face kept cropping up in my dreams that night, haunting me, and I knew I was soon going to have to start a serious campaign to forget him . . .

Chapter 4

Next day, I was so early that I was the first to arrive at work and the door was locked. The office was on the second floor of what looked as if it used to be a private house, though I couldn't possibly imagine who could have lived in such an expensive part of town. It wasn't the kind of place that Lord Somebody-or-other would have lived in. It wasn't grand enough for that. The house was tall, about five floors, and terraced, with railings outside and a basement with dustbins outside the barred-over windows. Everyone's rubbish got blown down there by the wind, too, so I was glad the G.R. Agency wasn't located 'below stairs'. It wouldn't have been very pleasant in this weather.

I had intended to look like a normal human being today and wear a strappy tee-shirt and summer skirt, but Mum had insisted I bring a jacket – 'in case the weather changes, dear.' Honestly, anyone with two working eyes in their head could look up and see that the sky was that perfect shade of deep blue which defies any trace of rain clouds. However, to keep her quiet, I'd changed my whole outfit and this meant that I was looking like *me*!

I spotted Sarah coming down the street, arm in arm with Joe. She raised her eyebrows when she saw me, though I couldn't tell if her expression was approving, disapproving, or just amazed. She herself was wearing sparkling white jeans which matched Joe's, and a loose top which was bloused out over a belt and looked very cool and nice. Whereas I . . . well, I was closer to Renaissance than medieval today. In warmer weather, I tended to adapt the costumes the men would have worn, rather than drape myself in long skirts – except in the evening, that is. Today, I sported a mid-thigh length tunic in pale blue cotton, with a belt I'd made out of dark blue velvet, and over my shoulders swung one of my favourite garments, a midnight blue velvet cape, lined with silver rayon.

Joe put about three keys into different locks, then pushed the heavy door open. 'None of the others are let at the moment,' he explained. 'Ours was the first to be converted, and they're gradually doing up the rest.

Someone's taken the floor above ours, but they haven't moved in yet, and the guy who actually owns the building lives in the penthouse at the top.'

'Yeah,' Sarah put in. 'We think he's a vampire because he never seems to get up till about five in the afternoon, which means he can't have got to bed till dawn.'

Joe riffled through the pile of post he'd picked up off the doormat. 'Phone bill,' he groaned, then added in happier tones: 'Hey, look, it's a card from Sandy! She's in Cliftonville. Her parents have sent her to a convalescent home to get over her op.'

'She'll get brown as anything, sitting out in the grounds in weather like this,' I pointed out, and immediately wondered if I'd said the wrong thing. I should have sounded commiserating, not envious. Still, the others seemed to agree with me, and I saw Sarah give Joe a funny look.

'Yes, it's all right for *some*,' she said meaningfully, then turned to me. 'He's off to Nassau soon. One of the bands is recording there. He won't take me.'

'*Can't*, dear, *can't*,' Joe corrected emphatically, while I looked from one to the other, wondering if their relationship contained more friction than love at the moment. 'You know the office simply wouldn't run without you, Sarah. We'd all go broke.'

I went and sat down in my little office and reached for the list of names and addresses Sarah had given me, which I had to type on to labels. For a moment I had a surge of panic, thinking I'd forgotten how to work the electric typewriter, because when I pulled the ON lever towards me, nothing happened. Then I glanced down and noticed it had been unplugged from the wall, probably by the cleaners. I plugged it back in and, after a few initial mistakes, my sticky labels began to coil out of the typewriter in an ever-lengthening roll. I was so oblivious to anything other than the clicking of my fingers on the keys that I jumped and hit my elbow hard against the wooden arm of my chair when the telephone on my desk jangled loudly.

It was Sarah. 'Could you do everyone a coffee please, Belinda?' she requested.

Sighing, I finished typing the label I was on, then took myself off to the dark cupboard under the stairs which served as a mini-kitchen. Then I realised I'd forgotten who took sugar and who didn't, and who liked their coffee black, so I had to go out and ask Sarah.

This time, I made sure I wrote everyone's preferences down on paper. Even if I was only going to be here for six weeks, I might as well do things properly, I thought to myself. After all, what would happen if my O-level results were rotten and I didn't do well enough to get into the sixth form? It would be nice to know I was in the G.R. Agency's good books, in case they ever had a permanent vacancy . . .

'Oh, by the way, Chrissy's in,' Sarah said, breaking into my thoughts. 'She says she doesn't want anything to drink right now, but she wants to meet you. She's in the office next to Griff's. And Phil, the accountant, will be in all day tomorrow.'

I wondered confusedly just how many people the firm employed, as I headed once more for the kitchen. This house seemed to have elastic walls. Every day, it expanded to produce another office, with yet another person I hadn't met in it. Were all pop music companies like this? It all seemed most haphazard, with odd bods wandering in and out whenever they felt like it. They seemed to have no structured work hours at all. In fact, it seemed a great way of life, once you rid your mind of all the things which had been dinned into you by parents and teachers about work meaning discipline, and turning up on time, and never being off sick if you could help it. But could they really make any money if they worked in this way?

The kettle boiled. It wasn't one which switched itself off, but I was so wrapped in thought that by the time I was aware of it, I was nearly choking in the hot steam. I jabbed my finger at the switch, then sloshed the water into the mugs, trying to remember who liked which one.

'The one with the nude lady on it is Griff's . . .' (I might have known, I nearly told Sarah as she was explaining to me) ' . . . and the one with the rude red tongue on it is Paul's. I like the red stripy one and Joe'll have any one that's going. You can take your pick of whatever's left.'

Why did even coffee-making have to be so complicated? I moaned to myself. I'd always thought the job of a tea-lady required nothing more than a pair of brawny arms for carrying a tray or pushing a trolley; I'd never have guessed it required a Ph.D!

I distributed the mugs, then tapped on the door I'd been told was Chrissy's.

'Yeah?' The voice from inside sounded decidedly grumpy and I almost walked away again, but the voice yelled stridently: 'Well, don't just stand there!'

'Er . . . I'm Belinda, the one who's doing Sandy's job,' I piped fearfully, poking my head round the door.

'Come in and let's have a look at you, then. I've heard all about your wonderful clothes.' The girl who spoke – well, *woman*, rather than girl, because she must have been almost Mum's age – was dressed all in black and had long, dark red hair which looked as if it had been coloured with henna. There was something about her which I didn't like, something cold and calculating in her narrowed eyes, an air of power in the confident, brusque way in which she spoke.

'Mmm!' she said, with a nod. 'Really unusual. There's a chance – just a chance, mind – that I might be able to get one of the teenage mags interested. You know, just a little piece on making your own clothes, with a couple of pics of you in some of your stuff.'

I felt my face grow hot. 'It's – it's not that good,' I stuttered. Surely she couldn't mean it? It would be wonderful if she did, but why should she? I wondered. I was nothing to her . . . she couldn't make any money out of me. Then I kicked myself for thinking such bitchy thoughts. She was doing her best to be friendly and I'd probably totally misjudged her.

'Thanks. It'd be great if you could,' I replied cautiously. I didn't want her to think I was some star-struck idiot who desperately wanted to get famous.

'Well, see you later no doubt, Belinda. I must make a few phone calls,' she said, and I realised I'd been dismissed.

I darted off down the corridor and cannoned

straight into Paul, the resident recording expert. As he was so short and slightly-built, only about my size, I almost knocked him off his feet.

'My God, you don't half zoom around!' he gasped, trying to get his breath back.

'Sorry . . . ' I gulped, realising I'd stood on his foot as well, to add insult to injury.

'If you really want to apologise, you can buy me a drink at lunchtime,' he suggested, with a hopeful grin.

'I . . . er . . . well, I only get my strict one hour,' I stuttered, wondering what on earth the others would think if I went off with Paul. I didn't want any of them to get the wrong idea. 'I don't drink, either,' I added lamely.

'That's all right. We'll make it an orange juice, then,' he replied perkily, and I just had to say yes.

Sarah shot us an arch look as we walked past the switchboard together on the dot of one.

'Don't you dare bring her back legless,' she warned.

Paul pulled a face at her. 'Don't worry, I'm on my health kick at the moment,' he assured her, and her pencilled and plucked eyebrows shot up, but all she said was, 'Stone the crows!'

'Sarah doesn't have much faith in my ability to stay on the wagon,' Paul confided as we walked down the stairs. 'But since I got my ulcer, I haven't dared to drink like I used to. At the record company, it was part of our job to wine and dine prospective acts, and we all took advantage of it. Some of us took *too* much advantage,' he added ruefully.

'You look fit enough now, though,' I observed.

'Yes, that's thanks to Lesley, my wife,' he said

warmly. 'She really looks after me.'

He proceded to tell me about Lesley, and about their little daughter, Emma, and he took some photographs of them out of his wallet to show me. It was funny, I would never have thought him to be a family man when I first caught sight of him in the office. But it appeared that, despite his tee-shirt, he was really quite conventional.

I thoroughly enjoyed the hour we spent in the dark little pub, chatting about all kinds of things. Then I looked at my watch and discovered it was past two o'clock.

'Gosh, I'd better zoom,' I announced anxiously, springing to my feet.

He accompanied me back, and as we walked past Sarah, he said: 'See? I've brought old Zoom here back safe and sound!'

That was how my nickname was born. It was heaps better than Bin-bag, I thought smugly. Though whether I'd ever wean Ian on to using it, I hadn't a clue. I had a funny sort of feeling that, whatever *my* feelings on the subject were, I'd always be Bin-bag to him.

Chapter 5

I might have known that things had been going just a little too smoothly, lulling me into a sense of false security, because the next day was total chaos, and all because Sarah hadn't turned up.

'Do you know how to handle a switchboard, Belinda?' Griff asked worriedly, then added: 'No, I don't suppose you do.'

He stood there looking helpless for a moment. 'It would be today, of all days,' he grumbled. 'It's not her fault, of course. Her mother's been taken ill or something. But it's awfully inconvenient. I've got some important international calls to make, air tickets to book, and two bands coming in.'

I couldn't help my ears pricking up at his last statement. So at last I was going to meet some of the G.R. Agency's mysterious clients!

'If there's someone who can show me what to do, I don't mind having a go,' I offered.

'I wonder if Chrissy . . . *hey, Chrissy?*' he bellowed, right down the corridor. 'Are you any good on the switchboard?'

'Get knotted!' Chrissy's voice shrieked back. 'If you think I'm going to be stuck out there when I've got—'

'Oh, Christ Almighty!' Griff groaned, and swept down to her office, leaving me dithering in the reception area, alongside a switchboard that was flashing and bleeping like Dr Who's Tardis. Moments later, Chrissy came up to me.

'Hi, Zoom!' she greeted me, grinning. 'I like Zoom — it suits you better than Belinda. You're not really a Belinda, are you? I've always pictured Belindas as sweet little mummy's girls in baby pink and blue and strings of pearls. You know, the sugared-almond types. But Zoom . . . that's original, like you!'

'Sounds more like a name a photographer should have,' I joked, thinking of zoom lenses. I was quite interested in photography.

'Sit down. I suppose I'll have to show you how this thing works,' Chrissy said with an exasperated sigh. 'I'm hopeless with mechanical objects. Even my hair-dryer breaks the minute I touch it, so you can expect a mushroom cloud to come out of this beast in about two seconds!'

I giggled as Chrissy flipped a lever towards her. 'That's switched it off night service and back on to ordinary working,' she explained. 'Now, if you hear a beep and one of these lights shows, it means someone wants a line – me, probably – so all you do is . . .'

It sounded so complicated that I never thought I'd grasp it, but I wrote down everything she said, though I felt sure I'd spend all day cutting people off.

'Think yourself lucky that it's not one of the big, old-fashioned jobs,' she said. 'They usually give you electric shocks into the bargain!'

She rustled off down the corridor, instructing me to ask her if I got stuck. Rustled was the operative word. She had an incredible dress on, which must have been an original Fifties designer number. It was black, like most of Chrissy's clothes, and made of taffeta, with a long waist and a skirt which belled out, and with stiff net petticoats beneath that. It had scoop armholes and a neckline which stopped just where Chrissy's cleavage started, which was lucky because I don't think she had one. Like me, she was skinny and long-bodied, but I liked to think people like us carried our clothes better than those with curvier figures, like Sarah. I still couldn't get over how amazing it was to be able to wear clothes like this to work. Chrissy looked as if she were dressed for a party, yet nobody cared or batted an eyelid. And as for me . . .

I'd really gone to town with my outfit today. At last, Mum had given up prophesying rain. It was really hot, so I wore a dress I'd modelled on a painting I'd seen in the National Portrait Gallery, showing musicians and dancers at a feast. Mum said it looked like something that had been found all ripped up in a dustbin, which annoyed me extremely, because I'd put a great deal of work into slashing the elbow-length sleeves so that they fluttered around my arms and created a lovely breeze when I moved. Dad, showing slightly more humour than Mum, called it my Battered Moth dress. Like most of my other summer clothes, it was quite short. I'd grown hardened to people staring at my legs. All the boys at school did, and I just ignored them. I didn't think there was anything sexy about my legs, as they were long and slim and my knees were a bit knobbly, so that's why I didn't mind them looking. It wasn't as if the sight of my pins could arouse raging passion in them, after all. I couldn't have stood that . . .

I'd taken the little headset off because it was a bit hot to wear on a day like this, and had placed it in front of the switchboard, when I became aware that a voice was squawking dementedly in it. I picked it up. It was Joe. 'You've just cut me off!' he howled. 'Can you get this number for me again, please?'

He fired off the digits so fast that I made a mess of writing them down, and had to ask him to repeat them, which made me feel a right twit. As the morning drew on, though, I found the switchboard getting gradually easier to cope with. It was very tiring work. I had no idea how Sarah managed to make it look so easy. She was really efficient, I thought admiringly. If I'd have been asked to type a whole pile of letters as well as look after the board, I knew I couldn't have done it.

Then Griff came through — for me. 'Belin— I mean Zoom...' There was a pause while he chuckled. 'Here's the number of the travel agent we always use. Now, I want one Club Class and one ordinary return ticket to Paris next Tuesday morning. Not too early and not too late, about eleven, if they've got a flight then. Tell them to put it on our account.'

I felt quite excited and important as I made the arrangements. When I'd got the details, I rang his extension back, thinking how weird it was to be talking on the phone to someone who was sitting only a few yards along the corridor!

'That was quick!' he said, sounding quite pleased. 'I've just realised I'll need a hotel reservation, of course, just for myself, for two nights. We handle this girl singer and pianist, you see, and she's got a week's residency in a Paris nightclub,' he explained. 'They've made arrangements for her to stay in a company apartment. I'm going over to make sure everything's all right, and I might as well stay an extra night to take in some Paris nightlife!'

Any nerves I'd had disappeared as, feeling like an old hand at the game, I got back to the girl in the travel agent's again. I was so busy that I'd quite forgotten Griff's remark about some groups coming in, and it wasn't until the door suddenly swung open and four tall, extremely good-looking black guys were standing there, beaming genially at me, that I remembered.

'We've got an appointment with Griff Roberts,' explained the tallest one, leaning his elbow nonchalantly on the top of the switchboard and nearly squashing the packet of sandwiches which Paul had kindly gone out and bought me, as I was having to work through my lunch hour. 'We're a bit late, though . . .'

'About three weeks late!' joked another of them, then added hastily: 'No, only about half an hour, really. He hasn't gone out, has he?'

'Nope. He's around somewhere. I'll see if I can dig him out for you,' I promised, grinning happily at them. They really were a laugh. I wondered what kind of music they played. Funky, probably. They reminded me of one of those American bands that did the great breakdance routines.

I got Griff, and he asked for them to be sent down to his office. Ten minutes later, he asked me to book a table at a nearby restaurant, then they all trooped off for lunch, leaving me gazing enviously after them. One down, and one to go, I thought, recalling Griff's remark about two bands being due in.

Things went quite quiet in the afternoon, and I was able to relax and eat my sarnies in peace. Chrissy came out and sat on the desk beside me, her absurdly high-heeled shoes dangling off her long, narrow feet. She saw me looking at them and remarked: 'People say narrow feet are aristocratic. What they don't tell you is that aristocrats can afford to get their shoes hand-made, but I can't. And you just try buying size sevens in a triple-A fitting!'

I sympathised with her, and she started chatting about her work. I gradually found myself liking her better. I still couldn't quite understand my initial, frosty reaction to her. Maybe my judgement was slipping, I mused to myself.

The second band arrived before Griff got back, and I had to tell them to wait in reception. They consisted of two girls and three blokes and there wasn't room for all of them to squash on to the leather sofa, so one of the girls sat on the knee of one of the guys, and the other girl and another bloke squeezed beside them, while the third boy perched on the table. I tried not to stare at them. They all looked a bit bedraggled somehow, as if they'd spent the night sleeping on the deck of a cross-Channel ferry in a high wind.

The bloke on the table got out some cigarette papers and began manufacturing a roll-your-own. It wasn't until he puffed at it a couple of times, then started passing it around that I realised, with a feeling of shock, that it wasn't just ordinary tobacco they were smoking.

Suddenly, a door slammed open down the corridor and Chrissy came hurtling out of her office.

'*Bax!*' she yelled. 'Put that out at once! You know we don't allow any dope here. We don't want to get busted by the police. Don't be so stupid . . .'

The one on the table, Bax, gave her a sulky look, stubbed the cigarette out in the ash tray and wrapped it carefully in a tissue before putting it in his pocket.

'I want you to come along to my office, anyway,' Chrissy added in slightly friendlier tones. 'I've got that new set of photographs to show you, and you said you'd never seen that piece about you that was in *Smash Hits* . . .'

They dutifully followed her, and after they'd disappeared, I found that I was feeling quite shaken. I'm no prude, and I'd never try to dictate to anyone about what they should or shouldn't do, but it was the first time I'd ever encountered drugs. Some of the kids at school claimed to have tried this and that, but I'd only thought, more fool them . . . However, when Paul came past on his way to the loo, and gave me a cheery wink and a grin, I felt a lot better.

It was just gone four, and I'd been trying for ages to get a number in New York for Griff that seemed permanently engaged, when I suddenly heard the door into the reception area swing open and became aware that four more strangers had walked in.

'Won't keep you a tic,' I promised without looking up, as I was in mid-dial. Honestly, my index finger was getting quite sore. I still didn't get through, so, with a muttered: 'Damn!' I looked up — and found myself peering into a pair of strangely piercing grey eyes that were staring just as intently at me. The face they were set in was one of the most perfectly chiselled examples of male beauty that I'd seen in all my life.

Chapter 6

I was aware I was gawping, so I determinedly set my lips in a firm line, then forced them into a smile, but I was still gazing at that perfectly sculpted jaw-line, the heart-breaking curve of his cheekbones that gave me a kind of ache inside, and the classically straight nose. His hair was like lemon silk. It capped his head shiningly, then swept behind his ears and stopped just as it touched his shoulders, where it curved under in an unbroken wave. He smiled and there was something teasing in the way his eyes danced.

'Is Joe in?' he enquired.

The other guys with him were also above average in the good-looks stakes, but they weren't arousing the weird little ripples and judders of feeling that he was. I hadn't seen Joe since lunchtime. 'I'll try him,' I said weakly, moving my arm to the switchboard like a remote-controlled automaton.

To my surprise, Joe *was* in. He must have come back from lunch during one of the few moments that I hadn't been at the board. 'Who is it?' he asked a bit irritably. I felt an idiot telling him I didn't know.

'Who shall I say it is?' I hissed embarrassedly, aware that the fair-haired boy's hypnotic eyes hadn't left my face for an instant. It was as if he were daring me to a staring match.

'Flip Sauvage,' he answered lightly, as if it were a common name like John Smith.

I relayed the information down the telephone, and was rewarded with a hearty: 'Oh, good . . . about time, too! Send him in.'

I didn't know whether or not I should warn Joe that there was more than one of them. In the end, I told them all to go to his office.

'Will you still be here when I come back?' Flip's question was so direct, it brought the colour flaming to my cheeks.

'I . . . I don't know,' I stumbled. 'I go home at half-past five.'

'Then I'll just have to hope Joe doesn't keep us too long,' he replied. Once again, he gave me that smile that was half teasing, half wistful, then set off in the wake of the others.

After he'd gone, I sat there in a daze. I was completely stunned. In a mere minute, two at most, my whole life had changed. New possibilities were staring me in the face, new emotions were whirling round inside me. I'd just never seen anyone like him, never been so knocked out by any boy on a first meeting. I didn't quite know how to cope with myself. On the one hand, I was angry that I'd let anyone get me all stupid and dithery like this. But on the other, I felt so full of excited energy that I could have danced round the office.

Was this what they called love at first sight? Was I being too hopeful in thinking he was interested in me?

Anyway, who *was* Flip Sauvage? He was so striking that I found myself wondering why I'd never seen his face staring at me out of magazines, or off the TV screen. Nobody who saw him could possibly ignore or forget him. Even if he couldn't sing or play an instrument, his face could have been his fortune. Maybe . . . and I found my pulses racing at the thought . . . maybe the G.R. Agency were going to be in at the very beginning of his rise to fame. Perhaps he had yet to cut his first record and pose for his first professional photographs. Perhaps, in future years, I'd be able to dine out on the fact that I had seen Flip Sauvage, the world famous megastar, on the very day he signed his first management and recording contract!

There was a buzz from Joe's extension and I flipped the lever and spoke into the mouthpiece, briefly congratulating myself on how quickly I'd learned my new role in the firm.

'Four coffees, one with sugar, and one tea, no milk, no sugar, and a slice of lemon if we've got any,' was Joe's order.

I prayed the switchboard wouldn't suddenly get busy as I hurried to the kettle. I couldn't help thinking that the tea must be for Flip. It somehow suited his grave, ascetic looks. There was no lemon, though, so I hoped he'd forgive me.

As I carried the mugs in on the tray, I could hear them rattling alarmingly as my hands shook with nerves, and I tried my best not to slop any of them. I put the tray down on Joe's desk and he muttered a brief thanks. I was just about to leave, forcing myself not to look at Flip, when I heard his cool voice ask: 'What's your name?'

Instantly, my head shot up and my eyes darted around the room. He *was* talking to me, wasn't he? He must have been, because everyone was looking at me. My brain began working at fever-pitch. Should I say Belinda, or would that class me as an 'ordinary girl'? Should I say Zoom, and risk them all bursting into laughter?

I took a deep breath. A boy like him would want an exotic creature like himself, not an ordinary little switchboard girl. Flip and Zoom . . . the names would sound great coupled in the gossip columns of the music papers. I could see our photograph now on the front page of the Daily Mirror . . . 'Flip Sauvage returning from Hawaii with his constant companion, the mysteriously named Zoom'.

'Just call me Zoom,' I replied, my voice, strangulated by nerves, coming out in rather a pleasing, husky whisper.

'I want that thing you've got on,' he said quietly, tilting his head back and fixing me with that luminous grey stare again, like moonlight filtering through a wisp of cloud.

'What?' I certainly wasn't whispering now. 'What do you mean?'

'What I mean is, I've got to have it. It would look fantastic on stage, worn with thick black tights and a pair of those thin suede boots with little patterns cut out of the suede. It would be the perfect wandering minstrel look.'

I looked around, but no-one was laughing; they were all taking him completely seriously. Obviously he *was* destined to become a big star.

'I . . . you won't be able to get one like it,' I floundered. 'You can't buy them. This is the only one in the whole world.'

'Well, take that one off and give it to me, then,' he suggested, in the same cool, serious tone of voice, though his eyes twinkled.

I was horribly flustered by now, and fortunately Joe came to my rescue. 'Stop teasing the poor girl,' he ordered warningly, then added: 'I can hear that switchboard bleeping.'

I'd forgotten all about the switchboard. Just as I turned to rush out of Joe's office, I heard the door of Griff's office being flung open.

'Where's that bloody girl got to? What about my call to the States?' he bellowed threateningly.

Then he saw me coming out of Joe's room. 'I'm sorry, I had to make coffee,' I apologised lamely.

'Well, I suppose you can't be expected to do everything at once, though you seem pretty good at it,' he owned grudgingly. 'Now, get me that call, there's a girl. I can't get on with anything else till I've spoken to Viv Sharman at the studios.'

Maybe I was mistaken, but as I walked away from the door of Joe's office, I thought I heard raised voices coming from inside, and I found myself hoping that Joe wasn't telling Flip off for bothering me. I glanced at my watch. It was ten to five, and I felt utterly drained and exhausted. So much had happened today, and I'd had to learn so many new things. How much could the human brain absorb in one day? I wondered. What happened when it reached saturation point? Did it just go fizz-whirr and give you an instant nervous breakdown?

The other burning question was . . . did I want to wait for Flip? Had he been just pulling my leg, trying out lines on me, testing his fatal charm? That would be easy to believe, but my instincts told me otherwise. They screamed that something special had happened, something that Flip had already acknowledged and was now waiting for me to confirm. That joking around in Joe's office had just been a pretence in front of the other men. I knew from many experiences at school that boys tended to gang up and joke about when an attractive girl – or even *any* girl, I mustn't kid myself – came along.

I was aware that at school the boys tended to look on me as something of an oddity, because I often wore my own outfits. I'd had dates, but nothing lasting had ever come out of any of them. When I was in one of my depressed moods, I'd tell myself that they were just daring each other to take me out and see if I was as odd as I looked. Anyway, most of them weren't very interesting. Except Ian, of course, and I'd never stood an earthly with him. It was horribly ironic that the boys you liked never liked you, and vice versa. It seemed like one of the great rules of life. Sod's law, Dad called it, though I'd never been quite sure what that meant.

At last I managed to get the number Griff wanted, and switched the call through to him. It was now a quarter past five. My heart began to beat faster. It was a race against time. I was determined not to hang around after going-home time. That would make it too obvious. Also, everyone would start asking who I was waiting for, and that would really put me on the spot.

Chrissy swept by in a cloud of perfume. 'Didn't Phil come in?' she asked. 'He was supposed to be taking me for a drink.'

I shook my head.

'Fancy coming for a quick one, then?' she enquired, then added, 'Oh, you're probably not old enough to do it legally yet, are you? Mind you, I was going in pubs when I was fifteen and nobody ever challenged me.'

It wasn't that I was scared of going into a pub at sixteen that made me hesitate to accept her offer, or even the fact that I preferred to wait a bit longer to see if Flip came out. The fact was, there wasn't much in the way of alcohol that I actually liked. Cider was okay, and I had the occasional glass of wine at home with my parents, but things like whisky and gin were just revolting. I'd had the occasional sip of other people's and just couldn't imagine how they appeared to enjoy it. Anyway, I knew my parents would simply love it if I came home smelling of booze.

'No thanks,' I muttered, trying not to sound ungrateful. I was also praying that Flip wouldn't emerge right now and act as if I was waiting for him. 'I – I'm going somewhere straight from work.'

To my relief, Chrissy didn't look cross, simply shrugged, smiled and went. Seconds later, I heard a voice singing a snatch of an old pop hit called, appropriately enough, 'Zoom', though I couldn't remember who originally sang it. I refused to let myself turn round, though I was trembling from head to foot and knew exactly who it was.

'Will you make me one, then?'

With studied slowness, I turned my head, but my smile was wavering though I was trying hard to appear confident. 'What did you say?' I asked. I was so surprised that I hadn't really taken his words in.

'I said, will you make me one of those things? Joe told me you made it, and that you were very good at designing clothes and making them up. Would it take you long?'

I eyed him up and down. In his thin tee-shirt and stretch jeans, I could see he didn't have an ounce of surplus flesh on him. He was quite willowy, and about four inches taller than me. The same size as I was wearing would probably fit him.

'Not very,' I replied.

'We're on *Top Of The Pops* next week and I'd love to wear it for the show,' he said.

For a second, I felt as if everything was going all swimmy and floaty around me, and I had to clutch the edge of my desk in order to hang on to reality. Surely he must be joking. He couldn't really want to wear something I'd made on *Top Of The Pops*? I wasn't even a good dressmaker! If you looked closely at any of my home-mades, you'd find places where the stitching was wonky, or the armholes were slightly different shapes, and I was hopeless at getting hemlines to look good and hang right. They generally came out like a child's drawing of waves . . .

'Honestly, Zoom, I mean it.' My vision cleared and I looked at him, trying to control my speeding pulses. 'It's recorded on Wednesday, so if you could do it by then . . .'

He gave me a hopeful grin. I just couldn't tear my

eyes away from his. 'I'll pay you for it, of course,' he added. 'Just let me know how much.'

'P-pay me?' I stammered, realising I sounded absurdly like the man in that 'P-pick up a P-penguin' advertisement that used to be on telly. A wave of doubt swept over me. I couldn't promise to make it for him by Wednesday. That would only give me the weekend, Monday and Tuesday! What if I messed it up and had no time to make another? What if it looked terrible on him anyway?

'You don't even know if it'll suit you,' I pointed out nervously.

'What are you doing tomorrow morning?' he shot at me.

My mind went blank. I had intended to go round to Karen's, like I normally did on a Saturday. Ian was usually there . . . but now there was Flip, and he was standing so near me, making my skin tingle all over.

'Nothing,' I said.

Chapter 7

'Belinda, have you gone off your head? Are you sure you've got it right? I just don't know whether to believe you or not,' Karen said dubiously, pushing her specs right up her nose, so that the lenses squashed her eyelashes – as if seeing more clearly would provide her with the truth.

'Of course I'm right!' I babbled hysterically. I'd dashed round to Karen's straight from work, after Flip had gone off to a rehearsal with his band. When I phoned her, she said she had something to show me, but I'd forgotten all about that in my eagerness to tell her my news.

'It's my first ever real commission – he really is going to pay me for it. He's promised!' I squeaked, grabbing her arm in excitement.

'Ow!' she yelled, and I let go.

'Sorry . . .' I said quickly.

'Promises, promises,' she muttered darkly. 'How do you know you can trust him? How do you know he's really going to be on TV, anyway?'

That stopped me in my tracks. I didn't really know anything about him. Karen had already said she had never heard of him, and she knew more about pop music than I did because Ian bought a regular music paper which she read, too.

'He wouldn't dare lie to me because he knows I could just ask Joe,' I pointed out, pleased with my swift resolution of the problem.

'Well, if it *is* true, I suppose I ought to say congratulations,' she said grudgingly. Then she brightened up. 'You know I said I had something to show you . . . ?'

With a flourish of her arm, she directed me to a large fish tank sitting amidst the jumble of books on the cupboard at the foot of her bed. 'The biggest one's called Larry, that one's Lily, then there's Lolita and Louise, and the smallest one's Lenny, though I hope he grows a bit. Aren't they beautiful? I only got them today — the pet shop ordered them for me specially,' she crowed.

I peered into the tank and recoiled in horror as something sprang and rebounded off one of the glass walls with a loud *ping*.

'Ugh! What are they?' I asked with a shudder. They looked like gigantic dusty brown grasshoppers with exceptionally large, strong, bristly legs. They were utterly repulsive.

'Locusts!' Karen informed me with a self-satisfied smirk. 'I thought of taking a dead one with me to the Youth Club, to illustrate my talk, but then I decided that a live one would be much better.'

'You'll clear the room in ten seconds flat if they see that thing,' I remarked stoutly. 'You needn't think I'm coming with you. It beats me how you can bear to sleep, knowing those things are in the room with you. If the cover came off, one might jump into your mouth in the night and choke you!'

'That'd be *awful*,' she wailed tragically, but just as I thought I'd got her converted to my cause, she added: 'I wouldn't want to *kill* it!'

I gave up. I told her I had to get home as Mum was expecting me to eat with her and Dad. As I left, I caught Ian lurking in the hall, looking all spruced up.

'Oh . . . hi, Boring,' I greeted him — though actually he was looking quite good, in fashionable canvas jeans and a grey and blue sweatshirt.

'Hello, Bin . . . Belinda. You're not dashing off, are you?'

''Fraid so,' I told him. 'It's the call of the chicken casserole. I'm starving!'

Funny, I thought as I walked back to my place. He must have been waiting for that posh girlfriend of his. But it had almost sounded as if he wanted to talk to me. I was really puzzled, and half felt like going back, but I'd have felt a real fool if the girl had arrived by then, so I continued on my way, and let my thoughts wander back to Flip and sewing.

First of all, he'd asked me to come round to his flat, but I'd felt very awkward about that. It may sound silly, but, at the age of sixteen, I'd never known any blokes who had their own flat, as the boys I'd gone out with had all lived at home. The thought of going to Flip's flat afflicted me with an instant mental paralysis, as if someone had told me to thrust my fingers into a flame. I was utterly incapable of agreeing to go there, and felt a real twit because of it.

He'd stood, regarding me with a kind of amused grin, as I'd stumbled out various excuses for not being able to come into town on Saturday morning, such as helping Mum with the shopping.

'Okay,' he'd said when I'd dried up and was standing there biting my lip and trying desperately to understand myself. 'Just give me your phone number and I'll ring you and fix something up for later in the day, perhaps.'

So that's how we'd left it, and ever since, I'd been frantically psychoanalysing myself. On the walk home from Karen's, I thought I had the answer. It was because I was scared of being alone with him . . . but I hadn't a clue as to why, unless I was frightened that something one of us said or did might spoil the chance of anything happening between us. But what did I *want* to happen? I asked myself distractedly. Did I want him to take me in his arms and kiss me and say he'd fallen in love with me at first sight? No, that was stupid ... but the idea did hold certain attractions, though I felt quite guilty as I thought about it!

Naturally, I couldn't keep the news of my first dressmaking commission from my parents. Mum seemed really excited and even Dad looked quite interested.

'This could be a big chance for you, Belinda,' she said eagerly. 'Just think – he might pass your name on to other show-business people and you might start getting lots of orders.'

Dad frowned. 'Moira ...' he told Mum warningly, 'don't go putting ideas into her head. She's got two more years at school to do, and exams to pass. We don't want to encourage her to abandon everything in order to try and turn herself into an instant Mary Quant or something.'

'Oh, Dad!' I cried in exasperation. If anyone was going to throw cold water on any plans of mine, it was always him. Work, exams, good results – that was all he could ever think of. I reckoned he had a chip on his shoulder because Mum had done a college course and he hadn't. He was so old-fashioned, too. Mary Quant, indeed! Why did so many grown-ups get stuck in their own era? Surely they still read papers and magazines and heard about newer designers like Katherine Hamnett and Jasper Conran?

It was the same with music. Dad still played all his old Beatles and Rolling Stones records, and had lots of albums by some bunch called Crosby, Stills, Nash and Young, whose music was about as imaginative as the name of their band. How he could listen to that dreary, endless moaning about love and loneliness and seagulls flying across the beach, was beyond me. It was so wimpish! You couldn't even dance to it. It was all airy-fairy and unreal, though the Beatles did write some pretty good melodies, I had to admit.

I found myself wondering what Flip Sauvage's music was like. I had a feeling that it would be cool and cynical and chic and very *today*.

'What was work like today?' Dad asked, interrupting my musings.

'Oh, okay,' I grunted, not wanting to give anything away. I didn't want them to guess how I felt about Flip.

'Well, surely you did something other than sell clothes?' he probed. I knew he meant to be funny, but it got right up my nose.

'As a matter of fact, I worked extremely hard,' I snapped. 'It was awful. I had to look after the switchboard and I didn't even get a lunch break. I certainly wouldn't like to have to do that full-time.'

Dad raised his eyebrows and grinned. 'So the music biz isn't as glamorous as you hoped?' he asked, still in that annoying, semi-humorous tone.

'I didn't hope anything,' I muttered.

'Well, when I was in a group, it was nothing but hard work, I can tell you,' Dad informed me. The revelation was so surprising that I stared at him.

'What kind of a group?' I asked in amazement. 'What did you play?'

'Bass guitar. I was lousy – we were all pretty awful. But it was fun at the time. Our guitarist's father was our so-called manager. He was supposed to get us bookings, but the money always seemed to disappear — into his pocket, probably. It was really depressing playing our hearts out for two hours in a stinking hot, smoky pub, all for a fiver between the lot of us, which didn't even pay for the petrol we used to get there!

'Mind you,' he added, darting Mum a furtive glance, 'it wasn't half great for pulling the birds!'

'*Graham!*' Mum exclaimed, looking shocked, and Dad sniggered.

'It's okay, I didn't know her in those days. We didn't meet until I'd swapped my bass for a clapped-out motor scooter,' he said, and they both laughed.

'I'll never forget that scooter,' Mum began. 'Do you remember that night when—'

'I'm just going to see if there's anything decent on telly,' I muttered, and left them to it. I went into the other room and switched the box on and flipped from station to station. A useless chat show, a stupid quiz, a dreary serial . . . and an old black-and-white movie with Humphrey Bogart. I settled back on the sofa to watch it, revelling in the clothes, the clipped, witty speech, the absurd situations. They really had style in those days, I thought. I could just see Flip as a first world war fighter pilot, in scarf and goggles, posing by a plane festooned in crosses to denote how many enemy planes he'd wiped out, languid, untroubled, yet hiding a deep sensitivity that he'd only reveal to the odd one or two people he allowed to get close to him. His best friend . . . and me.

Mum and Dad are best friends, I thought suddenly, and it was like entering a new dimension. They both had vague friends of their own sex, whom they saw occasionally, but they were happiest together. I suddenly felt hideously envious of them. How could they still be so happy together after all this time? Right now, they were in the other room, busy reliving old times, perhaps even finding out new things about each other, things they'd never thought to tell each other before. Their relationship was so close and strong that, at times like this, I felt excluded and unnecessary.

I sighed and glowered to myself as the film flickered on. Why couldn't *I* find someone who'd love me and stick to me for as long as they'd stuck to each other. Maybe I never would, I thought gloomily. Maybe Karen's first suspicion that Flip wasn't serious was right.

Suddenly, without planning it, I leapt off the sofa, strode angrily over to the telly and switched it abruptly off.

'I'm going to bed,' I yelled through the dining room door.

I went up to my bedroom and shut myself in, and almost immediately a wave of pure, cold despair washed over me. I didn't know what I was crying for. It was almost as if I was crying over a future which I'd already glimpsed and found to be empty and cruel, promising everything and then rejecting me totally. Nobody was really interested in me or my aims and ambitions, not even Mum and Dad. Nobody cared. At least Karen had her locusts to love, I told myself, breaking into a loud sob at the thought of how calm and self-contained she was. And Ian had his fancy, rich girlfriend, so even he didn't want to talk to me now.

That did it. I imagined Ian whisked off in that snooty

bird's car, being introduced to all kinds of snobby people with country houses and titled relatives. It was ghastly. He'd change beyond recognition. He'd absolutely ruin himself. He wouldn't be Boring Ian any more. My life seemed to be changing so fast, and I had no control over it, and I'd never felt so miserable in my life.

Chapter 8

The next morning, I woke up to find that my flaming period had started. I was furious. It always made me feel foul, with headaches and stomach-aches, and I was always worried about going out anywhere unfamiliar, in case I got caught miles from the loo and had an embarrassing accident. Why did it have to be today, when I was seeing Flip? I thought, cursing my bad luck. It was three days early, too. It just wasn't fair.

Mum guessed what was up and tried to cheer me up, as I came out with my usual grumbles about it not being fair that women should have to put up with this, while men had nothing similar.

Then Dad came in and colour rushed to my cheeks when I realised, to my horror, that he must have overheard.

'You only get that for a few days each month,

whereas we have to shave every single day, and it's a real drag,' he pointed out. 'You've no idea how time-consuming it is, and how sore your face can get.'

'You could always grow a beard,' I replied, as nastily as I could, because that's how I felt. It shook me to realise that Dad must have known when I'd started my periods. It embarrassed me horribly. I didn't know how Mum could discuss things like that with him. I knew I could never talk to a man about anything so intimate. I couldn't even ask for a packet of Tampax in the chemist's if there was a man behind the counter. Thank heavens for supermarkets.

'Belinda, could you just run down to the green-grocer's for me and get a cauliflower and two pounds of cooking apples?' Mum yelled from the next room.

That really put me on the spot. I didn't want to appear unwilling, but I had to be there in case Flip rang as I couldn't trust Mum or Dad to give him the right message. Then another thought hit me and rooted me to the spot in horror. If Flip did ring while I was out, he wouldn't ask for Belinda, he'd ask for me by my nickname, and Mum and Dad would probably think he'd got the wrong number!

I took a deep breath, and went into the kitchen, where Mum was busy dismantling the top of the gas oven and cleaning up all the places that had got covered in soup when she'd let it boil over yesterday lunchtime.

'Well?' she asked bad-temperedly. I knew she hated filthy jobs like cleaning the cooker and scrubbing the floor and what I was about to tell her wasn't going to improve her mood.

'I don't *mind* going to the shops, but must it be right now?' I asked, aware of a tetchy note creeping into my own voice.

Mum glared at me. 'Those apples have got to go into the oven within the next half hour, otherwise there's no pudding today,' she stated crossly. At weekends, we always had our main meal at midday.

'Can't we have something else? You know I hate cooked apple,' I grumbled. It was true. I couldn't stand the little hard bits from round the core that always got caught between your teeth.

'All right. You take over here and *I'll* go,' she snapped, straightening up and offering me a disgusting Brillo pad.

'Dad's not doing anything. Can't he go?' I pointed out. It seemed totally unfair to me that women should always be expected to do the shopping, while men were allowed to sit around undisturbed.

'Your father's been at work all week. Don't you think he deserves a chance to relax at weekends?' Her eyes were flashing danger signals, and I knew I should beware in case we ended up having a full-scale row. But I still couldn't help pointing out, unwisely, that I, too, had been at work all week.

'When you're doing a proper job and earning your keep,' Mum said acidly, 'then you can do whatever you like, when you like. But for now, surely it's not too much to ask you to stir your stumps and do the occasional bit around the house to earn your living?'

I sighed deeply. The trouble was, I knew she was right. 'Okay, I'll go,' I agreed unwillingly. 'But if anyone rings up and asks for someone called Zoom, that's me. I don't want you to think—'

'*Zoom?*' Mum interrupted. 'Who, or rather, what, is Zoom? It sounds like a new brand of wasp killer!'

'It's the nickname I've been given at work,' I replied affrontedly. 'It's because I zoom around so much.'

Mum started to laugh. 'Is it a bird? Is it a plane? No, it's Bat-Belinda!' she sniggered. 'Zoom, indeed. I hope you don't expect us to start calling you that.'

'I don't expect *you* to start doing *anything*,' I hurled sarcastically, and grabbed a carrier bag out of the cupboard. 'Tell him to ring back in fifteen minutes,' I ordered her.

As I stomped off down the street, I felt totally upset and at odds with the world. Nothing was going right. I should have been feeling all excited about Flip phoning, but parents and period combined had ruined it for me.

There was a huge queue in the greengrocer's and I was there for ages, glancing anxiously at my watch every half minute or so. I got what Mum wanted and dashed back, praying that he hadn't phoned.

'Is that all they had? It's not a very big one,' Mum grumbled, inspecting the cauliflower. Before I could open my mouth to say a word, she informed me: 'Nobody's rung.'

From willing him not to phone, I now found myself wishing fervently that he would. Ten-thirty . . . ten forty-five. Just before eleven, the phone jangled and I belted off to answer it, but Dad got there first and my heart sank as I realised it was the bloke from the garage where Dad got our car serviced. That meant he'd be on for ages. I lurked in the hall, getting more and more agitated as Dad gabbled on about sparkplugs and wheel bearings. I just knew Flip would be trying to get through, and would eventually give up. How could Dad do this to me?

Mum called me and asked me to dust my room, and I was actually glad of being given something to do, to take my mind off my awful suspense. Finally, it was lunchtime and he still hadn't rung. So much for his promises, I thought glumly. How could anyone be so cruel as to raise my hopes like that? So much for wearing my shirt on *Top of the Pops*! I sneered. I might have known it was all too good to be true. Blast Karen! Why did she always have to be right?

'Belinda . . . phone for you!' Dad yelled up the stairs. I'd been poring over a book of illustrations from *Vogue* magazine that I'd been given for Christmas, and hadn't even heard the phone. It was incredible!

I galloped down the stairs and snatched up the receiver. 'Hello?' I gasped.

'Oh, hi, Belinda. Doing anything tonight?'

Would you believe it, it was only Jen, one of the girls in my class at school. Fate was really torturing me today. We'd done *King Lear* at school and I found myself remembering the bit about us being like flies to the gods, who played with us and killed us for fun, like we swatted flies. It was so true.

Jen was inviting me to an impromptu party, but I couldn't commit myself as, for all I knew, Flip might want to see me.

'Karen and Ian are coming,' Jen informed me, as if that was an added inducement.

'I'm not sure if I can make it. I'll try,' I promised.

By the evening, I had a blistering headache and Flip still hadn't phoned. Karen rang to ask if I was going to the party and I told her I wasn't feeling well.

'Oh dear, sorry to hear that. We'll miss you,' she said. I assumed she meant everyone at the party, and almost laughed out loud to think of a bunch of my schoolmates missing me when they saw me every day of term.

'Is it about this commission of yours, dear?' Mum asked sympathetically, as I dragged around the house with a face like a wet fortnight. 'I thought that maybe you were building up your hopes a bit high. I'm very sorry for you if you've been let down. Life tends to be like that, unfortunately . . .'

'But he *wouldn't* let me down!' I shouted. 'He's not like that, I'm sure he's not!'

She maintained a tactful silence. The phone rang right then and I jumped, feeling as if it was jangling right inside my head, inside my very nerves.

'I'll get it,' I shrieked, my headache forgotten.

'Hello? Zoom?' There was no mistaking that light, cool, clipped voice, and my heart started to beat so quickly that I was worried in case I fainted. My hand went all weak and would hardly support the receiver.

'Yes, it's me,' I said, forcing my voice beyond a whisper.

'Sorry I didn't ring this morning. I had to rehearse. This is the first chance I've had to ring all day. About that shirt . . . I've been thinking. There's no need to try yours on, I'm sure it'll be all right. I'm good at being able to pick things that'll suit me. I'm thirty-eight inches around the chest, but it's pretty loose, isn't it?

Just as long as you get the shoulders right. Make the sleeves quite long, then you can shorten them if necessary. I'll come to the office on Tuesday afternoon, if you can have it ready by then.'

'Y-yes, of course. I'll start on it right away,' I heard myself babbling. I just hoped I'd have enough material left over from mine. I'd bought lots as it had been an enormous piece I'd found in a sale.

'See you on Tuesday, then. I'm looking forward to it,' he said. ''Bye, then.'

''Bye,' I echoed, and heard the click of the phone being replaced at his end. Oh, if only he hadn't gone, I thought. If only he'd wanted to chat, told me more about himself, let me into his life a bit more. This had been too much like a business transaction and now I felt flat, in a state of complete anti-climax. But he'd said he was looking forward to seeing me, I reminded myself.

I tore upstairs, cleared all the clutter off my bedroom floor, spread the material out, got my tape measure, and began work. As the smooth material began to take shape beneath my fingers, I thought of how it would look moulded against Flip's body, the wide sleeves billowing out, the fringes fluttering like streamers. I picked up the material and nuzzled my face against it, imagining Flip was already inside it, holding me in his arms. Suddenly, life was looking a whole lot better.

Chapter 9

It didn't really seem as if I was starting my second week of work. I already felt as if I'd been there for months. I'd had an awful job getting up that morning. Sunday was frustratingly busy and I hardly had any time to myself. I'd briefly switched my light off when Mum and Dad went to bed, so that they wouldn't get suspicious, then switched it back on again and worked till I had the complete shirt cut out and tacked together. I was much too tired to try it on and see if it looked all right. I just collapsed into bed, and really yelled at Mum when she tried to wake me up.

Sarah was back, which pleased me no end. It meant I could retreat into my cubby-hole of an office and sort out more boxes without having to talk to anyone.

I yawned my way through the day, then staggered home, ate a quick meal, then got back to work again. By ten-thirty, I had the shirt all sewn up, and was sitting up in bed, tidying all the ends of cotton. I felt quite pleased with my efforts. Flip's shirt had turned out even better than the one I'd made for myself.

Next morning, I got up a bit early, got the ironing board out, and gave the shirt a good pressing, then, discarding all the Woolworths and Sainsburys carrier bags in the cupboard, I rummaged until I found one that was slightly classier, from a big store in town. I knew I was taking things to extremes, but I was fussy enough to want to pay attention to details like that.

It was awfully quiet at work. Griff had gone to Paris, Paul was out, Joe wasn't in, and the morning began with just Sarah and me holding the fort. She was in a rotten mood about Joe's forthcoming trip to the recording studio in the Bahamas.

'I'd be really jealous, too,' I said, sympathising with her. 'But if you keep nagging him and moaning, it won't get you anywhere. Why don't you tell him you're planning a trip somewhere glamorous with some girlfriends of yours, while he's away? That'll get him going!'

I'd never thought I was good at giving advice, but Sarah looked at me as if I were a genius. 'Mmm!' she murmured admiringly. 'That's not a bad idea.'

Then Chrissy came in and announced she had to ring round the music papers and make sure they all watched Flip on TV on Thursday. 'I'm thinking of putting out a little publicity story about his clothes having been made by an unknown sixteen-year-old schoolgirl,' she said breezily. 'You've always got to think up an extra angle to get your artists noticed these days.'

I wasn't sure I liked being an 'extra angle', as she put it, so I shrugged and pretended I didn't have any feelings on the subject. Then I felt guilty for not having acted all grateful and enthusiastic. I was, really. But I still found it hard to believe what was happening to me.

Griff had left me a pile of letters to type, and I waded slowly through them, my eyes constantly straying to the carrier bag next to my desk, my ears flapping for sounds of visitors. Flip hadn't said what time he was coming in.

At lunchtime, I slipped out and went to the Royal Academy, which wasn't far away. I wandered round, looking at pictures, and after buying a couple of postcards in the foyer, I returned to the office. Today, for the first time, I was almost resenting having to be at work. If I'd been at home, I'd have been able to give Flip's shirt a really good inspection, neaten it up a bit more, maybe put some binding along the edges of the seams. Then I could have come into town and met him at a café somewhere, far away from the nosy people in the office.

He breezed in at about five, just as I was giving up hope, and my heart gave that now familiar thump when I saw him framed in the doorway.

'I've done it . . . it's here,' I croaked nervously, handing him the bag.

He went off with it, and came back wearing the shirt, which he'd slung a belt round and bloused it out over the top. He looked fabulous, like a kind of Cossack, but the look wasn't quite right for that shirt.

'What are the rest of your group going to wear for the programme?' I asked him, an idea forming at the back of my mind.

'We don't really have an image, as a group . . .' he began, but I cut in with: 'Why not?'

He frowned, then said: 'Because we're not really a band, I suppose. I'm the star, and they're my backing musicians, so I'm the only one who dresses up. They just wear jeans and tee-shirts.'

'Well, I think that's wrong,' I brought out, before I could stop myself, then stared at him fearfully. What a cheek I'd got! What on earth would he think of me, a mere temporary office worker, a schoolgirl on holiday, daring to suggest that a group who'd done well enough to be asked to appear on *Top of the Pops* should alter their image?

He leaned against the doorframe, one hand on his hip, and grinned lazily at me. 'Did you have something in mind?' he enquired coolly.

I was flustered now. I didn't even know what their music was like, so how *could* I think up any ideas for them. 'Forget it,' I muttered.

'No, go on – I'm interested,' he urged.

'I – I . . . well, what kind of number are you singing on the show?' I stammered.

He gazed at me with a shocked expression. 'You mean you haven't heard our record?' he asked.

I shook my head. Suddenly, he walked towards me, grabbed my hand and hauled me out into the corridor. 'Joe'll have a copy in his room,' he informed me.

His grip was firm, his hand dry and warm. I felt my palm tingling. What if someone should come and find me shut in Joe's office with Flip, I wondered, scared stiff. They'd think I wasn't working . . . I'd get the sack!

He found the record and placed it on Joe's turntable. Even before it started, I was worried in case I mightn't like it. It began with metallic percussion sounds – *ping, ping*, like Chinese music. Then a guitar came in, but sounding really weird, and then something that could have been a synthesiser. Then Flip began singing, in an almost-whisper, but it was so sexy. I shut my eyes for a moment, then opened them again, wide. To think I was standing only inches away from the man who'd made this record — was it really happening?

The lyrics were hard to make out, but they seemed to be about summer and cool breezes and sun-kissed bodies and love, but there was nothing sloppy about it — it was great!

'What do you think, Zoom? Will it *zoom* to the top of the charts?' Flip asked me, in his teasing drawl.

'I'm no expert, but I love it!' I assured him staunchly.

'Do you . . .?' He regarded me with his head on one side, and I wasn't quite sure what he meant. Suddenly, there was silence between us. The door was shut, we were alone in the office, we were looking at each other, and those shining grey eyes seemed to be drawing me towards him . . .

'Oh, *there* you are — I've been looking everywhere for you!' The cross voice grated on my ears. I wanted to lash out in fury at whoever had spoilt this magical moment. It was Chrissy. 'I've got a journalist on the phone who'd like a few words with you,' she told Flip.

'Tell him I'm busy right now,' he replied.

'No I will not! You can't start acting like that with the music press till you're a really big name, and you could hardly call Flip Sauvage that right now,' she pointed out, rather snidely I thought.

He scowled at her. 'Okay, okay, tell him I'm coming,' he agreed. Then he turned back to me. 'How do you think the shirt looks?'

Automatically, I reached towards him, then checked myself. 'It's that belt,' I said. 'It's all wrong. Just wear it loose.'

He unbuckled the black leather belt and took it off. I studied him. '*I* know what it needs!' I announced suddenly. His shirt had some extras that mine didn't, in the way of some coloured ribbon mingling with the cream-coloured fringes on the sleeves. 'If I sewed matching ribbons together and made a belt out of them—'

'There isn't time,' he pointed out, with a disappointed grimace. 'I've got to be at the studio at eleven-thirty tomorrow morning.'

I had a brainwave. 'The TV Centre's in Wood Lane, isn't it? That's not far from me. Perhaps I could leave the belt at the reception desk for you . . .'

It was the second time that day that someone had looked at me as if I'd just solved the mystery of the universe.

'I've got an even better idea than that,' he said. 'Why don't you come along to the rehearsal with me? Surely they wouldn't miss you here, just for a morning? Chrissy's coming and lugging along a couple of journalists. I'll tell her to arrange it and say you're the band's dresser or something. It's pretty hard to get people in, but it would be fabulous if you could make it . . .'

The look in his eyes made my insides feel like melting ice cream, without the chill. *Me*? I thought incredulously. At *Top of the Pops*? None of my friends would believe it! I wanted to fly to the telephone immediately and tell the whole world. Then my spirits sank as I came back to reality and realised there was no way I'd be allowed to go. When Griff came back, he'd be furious. He'd think I'd turned into exactly the sort of girl he didn't want to employ.

'See you in a minute,' Flip promised, and went off in search of Chrissy. It was now nearly half-five, so I plodded into my office and began to get my things together. Then I realised Flip hadn't mentioned paying me for the shirt. Almost as soon as I'd thought it, I told myself off for being mean and mercenary. It was enough to see him wearing it on TV. I didn't want money. But I did very much want to go to the TV studios. I felt like a small kid who'd been half-promised a treat, but had to wait to see what the weather was like, or if Mum was in the mood.

I didn't dare go home as there was still the matter of the belt to be settled. Sarah yelled goodbye and I hung around and made myself a cup of tea. It was nearly six o'clock before Chrissy's door opened and she and Flip came out and caught me standing in the corridor.

Flip grinned. 'It's all fixed for tomorrow!' he told me cheerily.

'What do you mean?' I asked weakly. I didn't believe that dreams could come true. Not to me, anyway.

'Chrissy's told them at the Beeb that my costume isn't finished and that you, as my costume designer, have to come and put the final touches to it, so you're to meet Chrissy by the main gate at eleven, and go in with her.'

'But what about work?' I protested. 'I can't just not turn up!'

'Chrissy'll have a word with Joe at home tonight. Don't worry, Zoom. No work's so serious that you can't have fun. Nothing's worth worrying about, anyway. *I* never worry.'

I thought I caught Chrissy giving him a funny look behind his back. Sometimes I thought there was an awful lot going on that I didn't understand. But it didn't matter. Not now, with so many fabulous things happening!

Chapter 10

I'd promised to ring Karen that Tuesday night, but though I remembered, I kept putting it off. I didn't have time, for one thing, because I had the belt to make. Plus, I was dreading her reaction to my news. She'd either go mad with envy and call me all the names under the sun for not taking her with me, or else she'd go all aloof and unbelieving.

I couldn't avoid her, though, because she rang me. It was an extremely embarrassing conversation. She chose the second reaction, the one of utter disbelief, and practically accused me of lying. I was furious.

'If you don't believe me, just come down to the TV Centre at eleven o'clock tomorrow morning and see for yourself!' I yelled.

'Maybe I'll do just that,' she retorted stiffly.

My needle worked about twenty times faster after that, hand-sewing the strips of brightly coloured ribbon on to the backing fabric. I made the belt deliberately too short, so that the four ribbons could meet in the middle and each tie up with the other end in the same colour. I hoped it would work.

Mum and Dad didn't have much to say about my forthcoming adventure, but they seemed vaguely disapproving. I really felt on my own, with them and Karen all against me. Still, I told myself defiantly, I was doing very well indeed with no help from anyone.

When I got to the TV Centre, which was a quick and easy journey from Ealing Broadway on the Central Line, there was no sign of Chrissy, and I started worrying in case she didn't turn up. Then, at a quarter past eleven, I spotted her leaping out of a taxi. She had an enormous pair of sunglasses on and was clutching a blue and pink striped briefcase. She said something to the security man at the gate, then the two of us were walking up the drive to the large glass entrance doors.

Chrissy was carrying on about some new club she'd been to the night before, but I was far too excited to keep my attention on what she was saying. My heart was thumping almost painfully. I was inside the BBC TV Centre – I could hardly believe it! – and somewhere in the building Flip would be waiting. But was he looking forward to seeing *me*? How could I ever find out whether or not he was just indulging me, giving a little schoolgirl a treat, or whether he took me seriously as an adult, a potential girlfriend, even? I remembered the way he'd listened so keenly when I'd talked to him, gazing at me levelly with his dizzying grey eyes.

Chrissy spoke to a man at the long reception desk, then we went round a corner and up in a lift. We went down a corridor, up to a door – and then we were halted by a girl in a jumpsuit so pink that it was almost luminous. It made a daring clash with her vivid orange hair. She asked us who we were, Chrissy told her, and then she led us into a large, noisy room which I didn't recognise at first. Then suddenly I did. Empty of leaping, cheering crowds, it looked completely different, but I knew it was the studio I saw on telly every week, the studio where *Top of the Pops* took place, and I felt an excited tingle run right through me.

Chrissy waved to three blokes who came over. I recognised them as Flip's band, and Chrissy introduced each one to me; Jake, the guitarist, Rod, who played bass guitar, and Stu, the drummer.

'He's not here,' Jake said, sounding cross. 'He'd better get here soon. We're on fourth.'

'Rod, go to the dressing room, see if he's shown up yet,' Chrissy ordered.

'What happens this morning, then?' I asked her, fascinated by the cameras that moved around and swung about like mechanical animals, their operators perched on them, looking most precarious. 'Are that group up there actually playing or what?' I'd asked that because I could see a boy playing a guitar without any electric lead or microphone near it.

'The people appearing on the programme all rehearse where they're going to stand and how they're going to move, so that the director can get the camera angles worked out, and the lighting people can organise their side of things. I've been to so many of these things, I suppose I take it all for granted now. Oh, and they're not playing, they're miming to their record. There's a proper run-through from about four o'clock to six o'clock where everyone actually plays and sings,' she explained.

'Oh, couldn't I stay for that?' I begged, then wished I hadn't said anything. Of *course* I couldn't. I wasn't a music biz executive like Chrissy. I was only a dogsbody and I had to get back to the office. However, Chrissy was saved from having to answer me, because a tall, fabulous-looking black guy strolled past and said, 'Hi,' to her.

'Hey, isn't that Jim Rivers from TLC?' I breathed excitedly.

She confirmed that it was. I looked round and spotted a pretty blonde girl who I knew was the lead singer from a famous American group as I'd seen her face in lots of magazines. None of my friends will believe this, I thought wonderingly. I imagined going back to school for the start of the next term and telling everyone. How on earth was I ever going to convince them I wasn't making it all up? Why didn't I think to bring my camera? I felt almost light-headed. Here I was, with famous stars all around me – and there were people like poor Karen, slaving away in shops and factories. Why should I get all the luck? Yet I *had* got it – and to top everything, here was Flip walking towards me, flanked by Rod and Stu, and walking slightly in front of him, almost tripping him up, was a very scruffy-looking bloke in stained plimsolls, grotty jeans and a frayed, grubby jumper.

Chrissy bounded forward and grabbed his arm. 'Hey – you were supposed to come and see me first,' she complained.

'He's a reporter from *Musicians Monthly*,' Jake explained in my ear.

I turned my head – and found myself gazing at Flip, who was grinning at me.

'Snap!' he said jokingly. We were both wearing *the* shirt – though I was wearing mine as a dress, as usual. 'You look as though you should be part of the band,' he murmured, his lips so close to my ear that I felt my skin tingle all across my shoulders and down my arms. My pulse was racing and I tried to think of something witty to say, but failed abysmally.

A girl came bustling up to us, said something to Chrissy and began to lead Flip and his band off.

'Hey . . . the belt!' I called after him. He stopped and I dashed up and handed it to him. He looped it round his waist and tied the ribbons.

'No, not like that,' I scolded, and dragged it to one side, where the trailing streamers looked so much better than dangling straight down the front.

The journalist was asking Chrissy things and making notes, so I moved away. As Flip and the band took their places on the stage, I became aware of a rather older man with a beard, standing a few feet away from me. He caught my eye and nodded. 'Are you his girlfriend?' he asked.

I was so astonished that my 'No!' came out rather too sharply.

'Oh, sorry . . .' he smiled. 'I thought that, as you were dressed the same . . .'

'I just design clothes,' I explained.

'Well, it looks good.' He paused. 'Have you got a business card?'

My mind whirled. 'I – I'm sorry,' I replied, shaking

my head. Who was he? Was he important and powerful? Could he get me designing jobs? 'I'll give you my phone number if you like,' I offered, then found we both had pens, but no paper.

'I'll get it before you leave,' he promised, and had to go because someone was calling him.

Right then, excited as I was, my attention was focussed rather more on the stage, because Flip had started to sing.

Entranced as I was with his voice, I couldn't keep my mind off the subject of how the band looked. They should all have been in black, I thought – all except Flip. And he needed to do more with himself. That song, with its slightly oriental air . . . He should have worn one of those small black hats Chinese men wear, and his face could have been made up in stark oriental fashion – pale, powdered face, dramatically highlighted eyes and lips. It would have looked great.

And then I was drawn into the song. Flip's voice . . . he hardly seemed to *be* singing, it was more like a sort of whispered chant, yet there *was* music there. But he was so subtle, quite the opposite to the raunchy, screaming heavy metal singers, yet much, much sexier in my opinion. His golden hair gleamed almost silver in the bright stage lighting. Then they started whirling coloured spotlights on to him and I watched my cream shirt turn to all the colours of the rainbow. It was very effective. It wasn't until afterwards that I realised that there were far more sounds going on than there were instruments to account for them, and remembered what Chrissy had told me, that they were just miming to the record. So I still hadn't really heard Flip sing . . .

They were up on stage for about ten minutes, moving about, listening to what the man Chrissy said was the director was telling them, and miming various bits over again. And all the time I felt as if there was some invisible connection between Flip and me, something nobody could see, nobody could feel, except us. I was completely aware of him in every bit of my mind and body. When he pretended to sing, I felt he was singing to an audience of one person only. I was sure he was looking straight at me, though I didn't dare move right to the front. And when he came off stage, he walked in a dead straight line – right towards *me*!

I wanted to open my arms and have him walk straight into them and place his lips on mine, all in one smooth movement. I opened my mouth to tell him how wonderful his song had sounded – and then that blasted journalist had to collar him and start asking stupid questions! I could feel tears of disappointment pricking my eyes. Flip had been going to say something important to me – I knew he had. And now it was ruined.

Dejectedly, I screwed my face into a grimace – and then I remembered the man who'd wanted my phone number. I asked Chrissy for a bit of paper and she ripped a page out of her notebook. I wrote my name and phone number on it, then looked round the room for the man, but couldn't spot him anywhere. That made me feel even worse. Nothing ever went my way, I thought miserably. *Nothing*!

'So your real name's Philip Savage?'

My ears pricked up at this bit of information the journalist was scribbling down. Philip Savage . . . Flip

Sauvage. Not that much of a change, yet it made all the difference. Philip Savage was so ordinary, it could have been the name of any bloke in an office, factory or garage anywhere. But *Flip Sauvage* ... that was a star's name! I could imagine it in huge letters on posters. I could see it on album covers. It was right for him, just as I felt a different person when I was called Zoom to when I was called Belinda.

'Right, everyone ... drinks? Lunch? BBC bar?' Chrissy suggested, having to yell over the racket a group I didn't recognise were making on stage.

'Are you coming with us, Zoom? You're not going back to the boring old office, are you?'

My heart gave a funny sort of jump as Flip spoke to me. I looked at Chrissy for a sign.

'Go in after lunch,' she said.

'As long as you think it's all right ...' I went on doubtfully.

'Of course it's all right,' Flip assured me. Then he took hold of my hand ...

Chapter 11

Bev, one of the girls in my class, called round just as the programme was about to start. *Oh, no ...* I groaned to myself when Dad shouted who it was at the door. I couldn't really tell her to go away. I wasn't as friendly with her as I was with Karen, but I saw a lot of her at school because she was taking the same subjects as me. But I was surprised to see her, all the same, because usually she and her boyfriend, Pete, were inseparable. This visit could only mean one thing – that they'd split up. But I didn't want to hear about it right now, with *Top of the Pops* about to start!

'Hi, Bev,' I greeted her rather mechanically, leading the way into the lounge.

'Oh, do we *have* to have that on?' she moaned when she heard the TV. 'I've so much to tell you.'

'Yes, we *do* have to have it on. There's somebody on it who's wearing something I made,' I told her, trying not to sound too big-headed.

That shut her up. Her eyes nearly came out on stalks.

'You've had your hair cut,' I observed. Her usual rather frizzy halo of curls had been chopped to within an inch of its life – but, with a figure like Bev's, no-one would ever mistake her for a boy.

She nodded, then started babbling: 'Tell me all about it. How did *you* come to do something on *Top of the Pops*? Come on, Belinda, you're pulling my leg.'

'I'm not! What's more, the bloke you're about to see wearing the shirt I made is my . . . my boyfriend.'

I knew it was a bit of a whopper, but I couldn't resist. In any case, *was* it really all that far from the truth? I wondered. I was still in a dream after yesterday. Flip had held my hand, not once, but twice – in the BBC building, and as we walked into the restaurant. If I concentrated hard, I was positive I could still feel the warm, light pressure of his palm against mine, and the slightly tickly sensation as he slid his fingers between mine, and laced them together.

I heaved a deep sigh. Bev was looking at me strangely. Then Mum came in.

'Would you two girls like a cup of coffee?' she asked.

'Ooh, yes please, Mrs Harker,' Bev replied enthusiastically.

'Thanks, Mum.'

Mum went out and Bev was still giving me this odd, fixed look, as if she'd seen too many horror films and was turning into an instant zombie.

'Are you really as blind as a bat? Do I have to spell it out?' she demanded. I was aware that she was very fidgety. She kept rubbing her hands together.

'Spell what out?' I asked, aware that I sounded crotchety. The programme had just started and I was desperate to turn the volume up.

'I'm not going to say a word,' she sniffed. 'I'm going to wait till you notice for yourself.'

The band with the handsome black singer had just finished, and I was sure it was going to be Flip next. I got up, darted to the knob, switched the sound up, and crashed back on to the sofa.

Bev made a noise like our old dog used to make when he sneezed, a cross between a snort and a splutter, and began fiddling with buttons on the front of her dress. I felt really cross with her. Why wouldn't she settle down and sit still and let me watch my programme in peace?

'*Well?*' she squawked.

'I've already mentioned your hair. It looks really nice,' I told her.

'*That's not it!*' she almost yelled.

'Ssh!' I hissed. 'There he is – look!'

'What . . . him?' Bev enquired doubtfully. 'You don't really know him do you? He's gorgeous!'

The camera zoomed in on a close-up of Flip's face and those luminous grey eyes were once more penetrating into my heart, which felt as if it was beating dangerously fast. Just in time, I remembered Mum's instructions to go and get her as soon as Flip was on, and I opened the door and yelled. She came racing in, calling to Dad.

'Don't you think we've got a talented daughter, Graham?' Mum said loudly, as soon as Dad walked in. I glanced in embarrassment towards Bev, blushing like mad. 'Oh, Mum . . .' I scolded her.

Too soon – much too soon, Flip's act was over and someone else was playing. I got up and switched the set off. There was no-one else in the whole world that I was interested in hearing. Mum and Dad went back out again and left us to chat.

'Are you worried about your results? I am,' I assured Bev emphatically.

She shook her head. 'No. It doesn't really concern me any more.'

'What do you mean?' I asked, puzzled.

She thrust her left hand right under my nose. 'Look!' she ordered. 'I've been trying to get you to notice ever since I got here.'

Now, I couldn't miss it. The ring was a great, sparkly ruby surrounded by diamonds.

'*Bev!*' I screamed. 'When did you . . .?'

'He asked me to marry him last Tuesday and we chose the ring on Saturday.'

'It's really romantic,' I murmured enviously. 'I always did think you and Pete were ideally suited to each other.'

She bit her lip and looked a bit shifty. 'It's not Pete,' she said quietly.

'Wh-a-a-t?' I screeched, leaping half out of my seat and bashing my knee on the coffee table. 'Well, who is it, then?'

'Remember my cousin Sylvia in Liverpool? The one I showed you the photo of?'

I didn't, but I pretended I had, just so that she'd get on with the story.

'I went up there a few weekends ago. Simon's an ex-boyfriend of hers and when she introduced us, well . . . Tell me honestly, Belinda, do you believe love at first sight can really happen?'

'I know it can,' I confirmed, thinking of my first ever sight of Flip.

She ignored me. 'Then he came down to London on a course and we went out and . . . well . . .'

She went slightly pink, and all at once, through some flash of insight, I guessed that Bev had already done what the rest of us had only giggled and fantasised about. But I needed confirmation.

'Have you and Simon . . . I mean, I don't want to pry, and you don't have to tell me anything if you don't want to, but—' I stopped abruptly as the true significence of her words sank in. She wasn't coming back to school next term! That could only mean . . . but I couldn't believe it! Not tatty-haired, scatterbrained Bev! I could have expected it of Sue Atherton, who always dressed so tartily and wore inches of make-up, but not Bev . . . I couldn't hold back the question, and it crept out in a kind of croak. 'You're not . . . not *pregnant*, are you, Bev?'

She looked insulted. 'Of course not!' she snapped. 'I wouldn't be so stupid.'

'Then why aren't you coming back to school?'

'Because Simon lives in Liverpool,' she explained slowly, as if I were a mental defective or something. 'I'm going up there to stay with Sylvia while Simon looks round for a house. He's got a really good job, you know,' she boasted. 'He's the manager of a menswear shop. We hope to get married at Christmas.'

'But you'll only be seventeen,' I pointed out. 'Isn't that awfully young to settle down? What do your parents think?'

'Oh, they think it's fine,' she replied matter-of-factly. 'They like Simon. Anyway, Mum was only seventeen when my parents got married, and they're still together and happy.'

'A miracle,' I commented. Then, aware of the black look Bev shot me, I suddenly realised that, as so often, I'd said the wrong thing.

I congratulated her, we chatted a bit more, then she went, promising to drop in again, and perhaps have a party before she left for Liverpool. After she'd gone, I found myself thinking deeply. It was weird, one of my classmates moving into a different world like that. It was as if we were all on a kind of ladder, each rung representing another stage in our development, and Bev had moved up one, leaving us behind. I'd gained the impression that she now regarded the rest of us as immature schoolgirls. If only she could really understand the sophisticated circles I was moving in now, she'd have nothing to boast about, I thought. *I'd* never settle for a bloke who was a mere menswear shop manager! Oh no. My eventual husband would have to have talent . . . charisma . . . fame. Everything about him would have to turn me on. And everything about Flip did.

I sighed from the depths of my lungs and exhaled loudly. I shut my eyes, reliving how he'd looked on TV. I wanted to ring up everyone I knew and say, 'Did you see Flip Sauvage on telly tonight? Wasn't he gorgeous? Well, he's my boyfriend.'

Imagine if I, too, could wave my third finger under people's noses and see their eyes go *zoing!!!* as they spotted my priceless ancient Egyptian lapis lazuli ring, circled with rubies. Flip would never choose anything ordinary, like a diamond. Bev was going to Spain for her honeymoon. There was nothing wrong with Spain. I'd been to Majorca with Mum and Dad. But Flip would choose somewhere far off and deserted, like the Seychelles. Maybe he'd have some big hits and earn millions and buy his own island, somewhere where he'd take only me. We'd hold hands as we strolled out of the cool shade of the palm trees, across the hot white sand to the little, rippling waves on the edge of the sea. His hand would feel gentle and warm, like it had done yesterday, when we'd gone for that meal that I couldn't eat . . .

'What's wrong, Zoom? Don't you like curry?' he'd asked, that strange, quick smile of his just twitching the corners of his lips.

'Y-yes, I like curry,' I'd stammered.

'Then why aren't you eating?' he'd probed, sounding genuinely concerned.

There was no way I could tell him that just sitting next to him in an Indian restaurant had completely robbed me of my appetite. I toyed with my chicken biriani while the journalist talked to Jake, Rod and Stu in turn, and Chrissy listened, prompting and directing when necessary.

Flip kept darting glances at me and every time I intercepted one, my innards gave a sort of lurch, and I felt sick. It was an awful shame, because I could hardly ever afford to go to a proper restaurant, and Mum and Dad didn't eat out very often, but I couldn't have eaten even as much as a few grains of rice.

Also, I was worried about being away from the office for so long. I felt sure Sarah would have something acid to say. I never had felt quite sure about her. She had it in her power to complain to Joe about me and get me the sack, whatever Chrissy said to reassure me.

I glanced at my watch. It was half past one and I knew it would take me at least half an hour to get to the office. I nudged Chrissy.

'Don't you think I ought to go?' I hissed. The journalist had Flip deep in conversation. If only it had been just me and Flip at the restaurant, and not all the others, too, I thought regretfully.

Chrissy nodded confirmation, and I stood up. Then suddenly Flip's hand was gripping my wrist, lightly, yet firmly.

'Where are you running off to, Zoom?' he enquired.

It was horrible having to remind him that I was an

ordinary office girl, rather than a genuine member of the music business like the rest of them, but fortunately Chrissy came to my rescue.

'If she doesn't get back, I'll have to carry the can,' she explained. 'The place can't get on without her. If Sandy doesn't come back soon, she'll find herself out of a job!'

I grinned gratefully at her. Flip gave my wrist a little squeeze.

'Doing anything Saturday morning?' he asked.

The room whirled and there was a strange singing noise in my ears, as if I was about to faint. 'No,' I whispered, so feebly I didn't think he could have heard me. But he must have done.

'Come shopping with me, then.' His eyes danced as he smiled that quick, perfect smile.

The words left my tongue before my brain had even had time to consider the question.

'I'd love to,' I said. And that's why I found myself standing outside Sloane Square tube station at midday on Saturday . . .

Chapter 12

I was in despair. About six trainloads of people had surged past me and Flip wasn't among them. It was now twenty past twelve. He wasn't coming – I knew he wasn't. I felt such a fool standing there, my royal blue tunic, bright blue shoes and canary yellow tights drawing curious glances even from some of the bizarrely dressed people arriving for their customary Saturday procession along the Kings Road.

My parents had told me that when they were young, the place used to be crawling with hippies and psychedelic shops. Then, towards the end of the Seventies, the Kings Road was rediscovered by the punks. Now all kinds of weirdos came and went every Saturday, and the area was thronged with tourists and foreign TV and film crews, capturing the strangest of them on film. They were nothing but posers, but everyone loved it. I longed to hurl myself into the colourful, fashionable throng, but only with Flip by my side. Otherwise, it would be like going alone to a party, to which you hadn't even been invited.

Twenty-five past ... I may as well give up, I thought. I was getting really agitated, because a scary-looking guy in leathers and chains, with a bald head and dangly earrings, kept trying to chat me up and wouldn't take no for an answer.

Then I spotted him. It *had* to be him. Nobody else could have that particular shade of golden hair. He was moving slowly, yet the crowd seemed to part before him. People were gaping at him, presumably because they recognised him from TV. He was wearing white jeans and a yellow and white striped tee-shirt and he seemed to glow, like a patch of sunlight. I wanted to dash towards him, but I restrained myself. *Stay cool ... * I reminded myself sternly. *Don't act like a fan ...*

'Sorry I'm late, Zoom. I woke up late ... everything

got a bit behind,' he apologised.

'It's okay. I was late anyway,' I lied, in order to make him feel better.

We fell silent and I could feel my shyness growing, so I forced myself to speak, thinking that anything, no matter how stupid or banal, would be better than nothing.

'So you didn't get the train?' I commented.

'Hardly. I only live ten minutes' walk away,' he said laughingly, and, once again, I felt I'd made an idiot of myself.

We began to walk up the main road. 'It must be nice for you, living so close to the centre of town,' I remarked.

His grunt of assent was lost in the roar of the traffic. I tried again.

'Where exactly are we going?'

'I've got this photo session. The record's starting to move and Joe's fixing a tour up. We need shots for the album sleeve, and for publicity,' he explained.

'If I'm supposed to be helping you buy clothes, I've got to know what sort of thing you're after,' I told him anxiously, hoping I sounded businesslike. I didn't want him to think I was looking on this as a purely social exercise, even though part of me wished that it was.

'I don't know . . . Joe hasn't a clue, he's not that sort of manager,' he replied vaguely. Then he widened his eyes and gazed searchingly at me. 'That's why I need you,' he said. There was a faint, almost beseeching smile hovering round the corners of his lips, and my heart gave a lurch.

'Th-thanks for the compliment,' I spluttered, thinking, quite inconsequentially, how well my yellow tights matched his outfit. 'But if it's a matter of image,' I went on, 'there's the whole band to think about, not just you. I mean, what do the others want?'

'The others?' Flip sounded surprised. 'I'm the star, baby!'

He said it jokingly, but my cheeks burned. *Why* did I always have to put my foot in it? Yet, argued a voice inside my head, if he meant it, then he was wrong. In my opinion, nothing looked worse than a group whose lead singer was distinctively dressed while everyone else was a bunch of scruffs. It looked as if they weren't a proper group at all, but just a bunch of session musicians who'd been booked for the night to back that particular singer.

'What colours do you think I look best in?' Flip demanded suddenly, coming to an abrupt halt outside a shop with a display of neon-coloured tracksuits in the window.

'Black, white, yellow,' I replied promptly. 'Your hair and eyes are so striking that you don't need strong colours. They'd only distract your audience. Except yellow – and that emphasises the colour of your hair.' I hoped my views didn't sound daft, but I've got very strong feelings about colour. I always have had.

'Mmm,' Flip mused thoughtfully. 'So I've done all right today, have I?'

I nodded and smiled, but my brain was still working on the subject of Flip and his band.

'There's two things you could do . . .' I began nervously, not knowing if I should go ahead and risk his criticism, or stop now and be a yes-woman to whatever he suggested buying. I really was on very shaky ground.

'Go on . . . what?' he prodded.

I took a deep breath. 'Well, you could either stick to the minstrel kind of image, the slightly medieval look—'

'That's your favourite style, isn't it?' he observed, and I felt sure he was laughing at me.

'At the moment,' I confirmed, slightly stiffly. 'Who knows what I'll go on to? But you . . . when I heard your record—'

Flip butted in. 'I'm sorry I couldn't get you in to the actual recording,' he apologised. 'I did ask, but the numbers are very strictly limited. I suppose, if every member of every group had his or her family and friends there, there wouldn't be room for a genuine audience! Even Chrissy had to wait in the bar.'

'It's okay, I understand,' I assured him, remembering how disappointed I'd been. 'When I saw you in the show,' I went on, 'it struck me that you might look really great in a kind of Japanese look. Black and white, wide sleeves, draped material, graceful, yet stark. Am I making any sort of sense?'

His eyes sparkled and he shot me his quick, amused smile. 'Of course . . . I know exactly what you're talking about,' he said. 'Come . . .'

With a dramatic hand gesture, he ushered me into the shop we were standing outside. It was called *Hi-Tek*, and there was no other term to describe the clothes. They could have been torn from the walls of the world's most modernistic art galleries. White shirts cut on trapeze lines, splattered with lines and blobs of brilliant colour; pants as wide as a clown's, patterned like the aftermath of a collision between two lorry-loads of oil paints.

They were great, zingy, space-age – but they weren't Flip, and I shook my head firmly.

'No?' he asked teasingly.

'Not quite . . .' I replied ruefully.

I noticed that the girl assistant couldn't keep her eyes off him and I scowled at her and prayed that he'd take my arm or hand as we walked out of the shop, but he didn't.

As we wandered up the Kings Road, I was constantly aware of girls turning their heads for a second look at my ultra-fantastic escort. I felt indescribably proud that he was with me. I longed to bump into someone I knew. Then, only then, would I have proof that everything I'd told Bev about, and tried to tell Karen, was true.

We passed a window full of expensive-looking fur coats, then an amazing shoe shop where I had to stop and goggle for a minute or two, then suddenly we came to a shop whose name I recognised from a magazine article I'd read. I knew the garments sold there were fiendishly expensive, and I felt a bit nervous when Flip stopped outside it. I didn't want him spending lots of money, just because of some loony idea of mine . . .

As I opened my mouth to protest, he laid his hand on my arm – just lightly, but it sent a kind of electric, bristling feeling shooting all over the surface of my skin. With that one gentle touch, he had me in his power. If he'd wanted to spend a thousand pounds, I couldn't have protested.

But he didn't make me feel guilty. He tried on a white cotton shirt – long, but not baggy, like the one I'd made – and a shallow, wide-brimmed black hat. When he emerged from the fitting cubicle with them on, I gasped. It was just what I'd had in mind, only better. Flip's looks would have made even a prison uniform look exciting and fashionable.

'That's it!' I exclaimed, and he looked pleased, and wrote out a cheque for them.

'Weren't you on *Top of the Pops* this week?' the salesgirl asked curiously.

When he said yes, she promptly asked for his autograph.

'Why don't you frame my cheque?' he teased her, then obliged by writing his name on one of the shop's headed receipt forms.

'Do you mind people doing that?' I asked, once we'd got outside.

'No, I like it,' he admitted. 'It makes me feel a star.'

We found a pair of white trousers that were like those worn by martial arts experts. Then I tried to explain to Flip all about my make-up ideas, but I realised his attention had wandered, and had the sense to shut up.

'I'm hot, I'm tired, and I'm thirsty,' he complained. 'Fancy an ice-cold glass of fruit juice?'

'Not half!' I cried. 'Where shall we go?'

We hadn't passed anywhere that looked like the sort of place which would sell such a thing.

'My flat's not far from here.'

His flat . . . I'd dreamt of finding myself alone in a room with Flip, but now I was about to get the opportunity, I could feel nothing but pure panic. Yet I let myself be guided through the hordes of window-shoppers and promenaders, down one side street and up another, until I found myself standing by the railings of a tall, narrow house with a blue door.

'Hope you don't mind stairs, Zoom. My flat's on the third floor,' he said.

I couldn't speak because I had a funny lump in my throat which kind of closed it up inside, so I just shrugged and tried to look eager.

Flip led the way up a red-carpeted staircase. There were pictures on the walls but it was too gloomy to see them properly. Then we came to another door, on a landing. Following Flip up the stairs had been an ordeal because I'd felt acutely aware of his being only a few inches away from me. I could see his muscles move beneath his tee-shirt. One slight stumble and my head would have been nestling against his back.

But now, thankfully, I could keep my distance while he fitted his key into the lock. He pushed the door open, then held it and motioned for me to go on in. I caught my breath. It was as if the threshold I was stepping over was far, far more than just the entrance to his flat. I was stepping into a new chapter of my life, a whole new realm of experience. I wasn't with one of my immature schoolboy boyfriends any more. I was with a man – a famous, talented one, too!

Yet my first sight of his flat was a disappointing one. I'd expected . . . I don't know, something different, a room with some sort of flair, some definite taste. But this was – well, ordinary. Anyone could have lived here. An acoustic guitar was propped up against a small electric piano, which lived in a corner between a bookcase and the back of the rather shabby sofa. What looked like a whole weeks' worth of newspapers lay scattered on the rug in front of the sofa. Flip saw me looking at them.

'My flatmate's,' he explained with an apologetic grimace.

I hadn't thought of him having a flatmate and longed to ask him who he – or she, though I hoped not – was, but didn't dare in case he thought I had a cheek.

The mantelpiece above the boarded-up fireplace was littered with old photographs and postcards. As soon as Flip had disappeared to the kitchen, I stepped forward for a closer look. Some of the postcards were from exotic locations like Miami and Hawaii. My fingers itched to turn them over and see who they were from. I had a horrid feeling that he had scores of beautiful, rich girlfriends. Yet if he had, I mused, then why was his flat so grotty? It didn't make sense.

Flip came back with a glass in each hand. 'Why didn't you sit down?' he enquired, in that coolly amused tone of his.

I knew I was blushing. 'Sorry,' I muttered, and plonked myself on the sofa, carefully sitting in the middle so that he wouldn't feel obliged to sit next to me. In fact, I was terrified that he would. I wouldn't know what to do. All I knew was, I'd be bound to do something ghastly and stupid, like spill my drink, or sneeze all over him, or generally behave like a stupid schoolgirl. This is ridiculous! I scolded myself. You're sixteen, not six! But there was something about Flip that made me feel like a silly kid. Perhaps it was his own laid-back sophistication — or maybe it was my knowledge of what he was, a talented musician, a TV star, a future tax-exile pin-up.

I managed to smile. 'Nice flat,' I croaked. It was a lie, but I just had to say something to break the tense silence. If only I could feel easier and more relaxed with him . . .

'It might be if I didn't share it with Del,' he grumbled.

'What do you mean? And who's Del?' I asked, relieved that it was a bloke's name.

'Oh, he's an old mate of mine. He's sort of our roadie,' Flip told me. 'Most of this foul old furniture's from his parents' house. They bought new stuff when they moved.'

'Where do they . . . he . . . come from? And you, of course!' I stumbled, feeling the colour flare and fade in my cheeks again.

'Hampshire. Portsmouth. Terrible place. I was glad to get up here, I can tell you.' Flip swung his legs over the arm of his chair and draped one arm indolently across the back. 'Yes, Del and I were at school together — but, apart from that, we don't have much in common. However, one tends to stay loyal to one's friends. One never knows when one may need them,' he drawled, raising one eyebrow in such a comic gesture that I giggled. 'I sometimes think I need Del like a hole in the head,' he went on. 'If he was only handy with the hoover, it might help.'

'My best friend's a girl called Karen. Do you know, she actually keeps *locusts* in her bedroom?' I informed him.

'Really!' Flip gave an exaggerated shudder and I giggled again, hating myself for doing so because I sounded even more schoolgirlish when I did that.

'I do think it's true that you should stick by your friends,' I said. 'There was this time when Karen got stranded at a—'

But I wasn't allowed to finish, as Flip cut in with: 'So how do you think I look in my new gear, then?'

I was immediately conscious that I must have been boring him. 'Really good,' I enthused. I hardly dared put my next question to him, but it was burning on my tongue, and finally, it came rushing out in a gabble of words. 'Do you . . . well, is there any chance at all that I could do your make-up for the photo session? Get your image just right? I mean, I could tell you what to do, but it's hard for someone else to understand. It'd be much better if—'

He swung himself back into a sitting position. 'Why not, Zoom?' he answered brightly. 'That's a great idea. I'll get on to Chrissy about it. I'm sure she'll say yes.'

He put his coffee mug down on the carpet. 'Hey,' he said. 'Would you like to listen to some song ideas I've got brewing?'

'Gosh, I'd love to!' I told him eagerly, thinking what an honour it was. If only Karen could be a fly on the wall and witness me sitting in Flip's flat, being treated to a private concert, I thought with a sigh. And what about Ian, too? He loved pop music. I felt sure he'd be impressed. Then suddenly, I had the strangest feeling that I didn't want Ian to know about Flip – or Flip about Ian . . .

Flip picked up his guitar and settled himself cross-legged on the dark red rug. He closed his eyes and began to pick at the strings, just isolated notes at first, then chords. He began to hum a melody and my mind followed its twists and turns, imagining a field in the sunlight, then a stream. Then, in that sexy voice that was little more than a whisper, he began to sing about a girl who'd been abandoned by the man she loved. There were just two verses and a chorus. I was just getting into the song when he abruptly stopped playing and opened his eyes.

'What do you think of that so far?' he shot at me.

'It — it was beautiful,' I faltered. 'Really lovely.'

'I must finish that one soon. Now, I started this one when I was in the taxi coming back from the Beeb. It's about the problems of living in the city . . . being unemployed. I know all about that. Listen . . .'

I obeyed. I couldn't take my eyes off his face as he sang. He was so perfect looking that it was as if he came from another world, one where there was no ugliness and everyone was as tall, slim and beautifully featured as he was. His fingers were graceful as they toyed with the guitar strings. When he closed his eyes, his long lashes fanned out against his cheekbones, making me yearn to run my fingers over them. His lips were mobile, quirky at the corners as he sang with little grimaces about disillusioned kids out on the streets. I wondered what it would be like to kiss those lips, just to brush mine very lightly against his . . . and immediately banished the thought. It was ridiculous! I mustn't have ideas like this. Flip would never fancy me in a million years!

But I was wrong. When I finally, reluctantly, announced that I'd have to get back as Mum and Dad were expecting me, a look of real disappointment crossed his face.

'Oh – do you have to?' he begged. 'Stay . . . ring them.'

'I can't. I said I'd be back. Mum will have cooked . . .' I explained desperately.

He shrugged. 'Oh well . . . But I'll see you again? I rather thought you might have some good ideas about how to get this rathole looking a bit better.'

My breath caught in my throat and I gave a little, choking cough. Then, suddenly, Flip's arm was around my shoulders.

'Are you all right?' he asked, sounding concerned.

'Y-yes,' I stammered, cursing my stupidity. I thought he'd remove his arm then, but he didn't. Instead, he tightened his grip on me and pulled me closer, so that I could feel his hard, bony ribcage against my shoulder.

'Come here, Zoom . . .' he murmured.

I was powerless to move. All the strength had left me and I felt as if I was in some kind of trance. My heart was thudding so hard that I felt sure he must be able to feel it. I prayed that I wouldn't do anything idiotic now, to mess things up. I could feel myself trembling and tried – and failed – to control it. How could I remain calm, when Flip's great, shining grey eyes were gazing into mine, and his face was coming so close that it was impossible for me to focus on it? So close that I could feel the warmth of his nearness, and could almost brush his skin with mine.

His face hovered a hair's-breadth away from mine while I stood there in suspended animation, unable to feel the floor beneath my feet, no longer sure if I was even breathing. Every millimetre of my skin was tingling. Without my willing it, my face was tilting up towards his. If either of us moved, our lips would touch . . . and then they did. He brought his lips to rest on mine, so gently that it was like being brushed by a butterfly's wing. His mouth was warm and dry. Then I felt a slight pressure, and found myself responding. At the same time, his arm tightened around me. His lips moved over mine, questing, exploring, while I remained perfectly still, a submissive captive, praying he'd never stop. It was bliss – sheer bliss. I could feel my mouth curving into a smile.

It was over too soon. Flip moved away, removed his arm. 'See you soon, Zoom. In the office, probably. You know where the station is, don't you? Turn left out of the door, then right when you hit the main road, okay?'

I couldn't speak, I just grinned like an idiot. My legs were all wobbly as I walked down the stairs. Kings Road must have been just as crowded as before, but I didn't notice. I don't think I'd even have registered it if Prince Charles and Princess Diana had walked up to me and said hello. The world around and outside me didn't exist – yet inside, I'd never felt more alive or aware in my whole life.

Chapter 13

'How did he kiss you?' Karen was demanding. 'Mouth open, or mouth closed?'

'Karen!' I exclaimed in wounded tones, my cheeks growing pink. I didn't want to discuss my relationship with Flip as if it were a specimen under Karen's microscope in the school lab! This sort of thing was the trouble, once you started letting someone else in on your secrets, I thought grumpily. If I'd never discussed previous dates and boyfriends with her, she wouldn't want to know all about this one.

Mind you, nothing much had happened on those previous dates. There'd been a bit of hand-holding, an arm or two round me, and the odd slimy or inept kiss, but nothing at all to compare with what was happening now.

'Well?' she demanded.

'What do you think?' I fired back. At school, we'd labelled girls who kissed with their mouths open as tarts. So I wasn't going to admit how the pressure of Flip's lips on mine had forced mine slightly apart – and I certainly wasn't going to own up to having liked it.

She'd given me a frosty reception when I'd arrived this evening, still slightly in another world after my adventure with Flip. She'd accused me of neglecting her, and leaving her out of things, and generally acted so hurt that in the end I'd felt obliged to tell her all about Flip, from the very first second I'd laid eyes on him.

'Anyway, it's not the first time I've been kissed,' I pointed out. 'What about Kev Taylor and Darren Jones?'

'They don't count – they're from school!' Karen said scornfully. 'This is the first time you've gone out with a real *man* . . .'

I supposed it was, really. Kev and Darren had only been a year older than me. I had no idea how old Flip was. He looked about twenty. Maybe he was even older than that! I thought excitedly. It made me feel really grown-up.

Something was different about Karen's room. Then I realised what it was; the tank that had held her disgusting locusts was no longer there. I asked her what had happened to them, and her mouth puckered into a rueful grimace.

'They got out,' she informed me.

'Oh? Where?' I enquired, hoping she didn't mean they were still hopping around the bedroom.

'At the Youth Club.'

'Oh, no!' My jaw dropped open in horror. I could just picture the scene, girls screaming and rushing for the door, blokes stomping round trying to find one and squash it, or else pick it up to torture one of the girls with. Karen's description of what had happened after the goldfish bowl she'd transferred them to had fallen off the desk was all that, and more. I laughed until tears poured down my face. I was screeching and gasping so loud that I didn't hear whoever it was that opened Karen's door, until I suddenly looked up to see Ian standing there, an amused look on his face.

'I think I must have missed the punchline, but it sounded good. You must tell me later,' he remarked. Before either of us could tell him that it was only the locust story, he said: 'Well, I'm off out now. Going to that new wine bar, Chimes.'

'Are you going with . . .?' Karen created a significant pause.

'Yep. Nice seeing you, Bin-bag.' And with that, he closed the door again.

'Honestly, I don't know what he sees in that Melinda — apart from her money!' Karen exploded. 'She's ghastly, all airs and graces and the tennis club and her aerobics classes. *Oh, Ian*—' Karen mimicked a painfully affected voice, '—*I saw a simply super velvet tracksuit in Harrods, and I just had to have it* . . . Ugh — she makes me sick!'

'She's not the one you told me about on the phone that time, who came to pick him up in her car, and you were laughing about it?' I enquired.

'Yes, that's her,' Karen confirmed.

'That means they've been going out for — for *weeks*!' For some reason, the knowledge didn't altogether please me. I used to enjoy my teasing chats with Ian, and now it looked as if he was always going to be out when I came round.

'I'll say one thing for her — she's smartened up his clothes a bit,' I observed. 'That white canvas jacket he was wearing was quite something.'

'He must have robbed a bank to get it, though,'

Karen said grimly. 'I saw the identical one in Bentalls for nearly forty quid!'

I spent the rest of the evening with Karen and, by the end of it, I felt our normal friendship had been restored. She told me that she'd arranged to meet Jen and Kim and some of the other girls from our class, to go on a picnic in Richmond Park the next day.

'We'd love you to come. I was going to ring you up about it, anyway,' she said eagerly. 'If it's as warm as it was today, it'll be fantastic. If you wear something backless, you might even get a tan!'

'I've got a great yellow tee-shirt with a vee back, and I'll dig out those khaki shorts I had last summer. I might even cycle down there,' I told her. I was really looking forward to it. Always, when it came to breaking up for the summer holidays, I swore that I wouldn't even think about school until September. Yet invariably, after a couple of weeks I found myself missing the girls – and even some of the boys! Missing the chatter and banter and gossip, the moans about homework and tests, the crushes, the poking fun at the teachers; the constant feeling that, with six hundred people crammed into one school building, something exciting was bound to happen.

But, as it happened, the pleasure of getting together with all my old friends was denied me, for the best reason of all. Just as I was getting ready at ten o'clock, Flip rang!

'Fancy going to Camden Lock?' he asked, while my brain was still reeling from the shock of hearing his voice. 'I thought you might help me choose one or two things for the flat. We could go up to Hampstead

Heath after — there's a crafts exhibition on. They have some nice paintings and jewellery. How long would it take you to get to Camden Town? I could meet you at the tube.'

I considered, my heart beating wildly. It was a dreadful decision to have to make. The girls would think it rotten of me if I didn't go; they'd think I'd deliberately snubbed them. Yet if I turned down Flip's invitation . . . No, there was no question about it. No way could I miss out on a day with Flip.

'A quarter past eleven,' I promised. 'I'll be outside the station. Look for the nearest patch of sunshine and I'll be in it.'

Then I was stuck with the problem of whether or not to phone Karen. If I didn't, and just failed to turn up, my name would be mud. But if I did, and told her the real reason, they'd spend all day gossiping about me and my 'boyfriend'. But then, I mused, Flip *was* my boyfriend, wasn't he? He'd kissed me . . . and today was our first real date! I felt sure the others would understand . . .

Karen was quite off with me on the phone. 'Oh, *I* see. Fellas have to come before your friends, do they?' she said sarcastically. I could tell she was going to end up a real women's libber.

Flip was already there waiting for me when I arrived. I'd rapidly changed from the tee-shirt and shorts I'd put on to go to the picnic in, and donned one of my own creations, a sort of toga affair in faded green, which left one shoulder bare. I knew I ran the risk of going home that night with one sunburnt shoulder and one pale one, but I also knew I looked good in the dress. Next time I wore it, I'd have to put it on back to front and bake the *other* shoulder.

He was actually waiting by the ticket barrier. Seeing him standing there smiling felt like the best moment of my life.

'You look nice,' was the first thing he said to me. Then he took my hand and we strolled up the road to the market, which was absolutely teaming with people. By the time I'd identified four foreign languages being spoken around me, I gave up. The fifth could have been Polish, Hungarian or even Russian; I couldn't tell the difference. Besides, we'd found a stall on which I was convinced I'd spotted two genuine art deco vases. My mum had one similar, and she told me it was worth quite a bit of money. The price label on these said five pounds each.

'If they're genuine, they're worth it – and if they're not, they'd still fool most people,' I told him, in a whisper because the stall-holder was right next to us. He took my advice and bought them, and we stole away with our parcel, giggling because we felt sure we'd got a bargain.

Flip was crazy, I soon had to admit, but in the nicest possible way. Being with him was pure, loony fun. At the next stall, he fell in love with a stuffed bear!

'Oh, Zoom, I've just got to have it,' he insisted. 'I'll put it right inside the door, so it's the first thing visitors see. It'll freak them out! Oh, look at his face. He looks like a sad old dog, doesn't he?'

'No, a sad old bear,' I pointed out, and we laughed.

'But how will you get him home?' I protested.

'In a taxi.'

'He'll never fit in,' I pointed out logically.

'We'll take him on the bus then. Do you think we'll get away with half fare, like you pay for dogs?'

'Double fare, more like,' I snorted. 'Though he's no fatter than some of the enormous women I've had to sit next to, who've squashed me right out of my seat.'

In the end, I managed to deter him from buying the bear, but I might as well have wasted my words because, deeper into the market, he found a very moth-eaten stuffed leopard instead.

'Oh, what style . . .' he breathed. 'I'll have a real Twenties and Thirties flat. You must have seen pictures from that era, of ladies with one of these on a lead, all draped in full-length versions of that thing you're wearing, Zoom?'

I wasn't sure if I liked my dress being referred to as a 'thing', but I wasn't in the mood to quibble. 'Who was draped in it, the lady or the leopard?' I chuckled. 'Anyway, I get the feeling that the ones in the photographs were probably real.'

'Well, I don't care. I can't have the real thing, so he'll do. I'll call him Leonard — Leonard the Leopard. Come here, Leonard,' he said, stroking the beast's head. Its shiny glass eyes gazed unwinkingly at him. One of its ears was coming off. I'd have to find some way of mending it.

Leonard put paid to our trip to Hampstead Heath, so I needn't have worried about sunburn. We bought a few more things, then had some lunch in a lovely café in the market. Flip was wearing his new white trousers, with a baggy black wide-sleeved tee-shirt. He looked great. People kept staring at him, then talking to their companions, as if discussing whether this really was Flip Sauvage, and should they ask for his autograph.

After I'd finished my slice of strawberry gâteau, which I'd been unable to resist, Flip reached across the table and squeezed my hand. 'You're fun, Zoom,' he said, and just those three words made the temperature around me, which was already hot, rise to about a hundred and twenty degrees.

We wandered out with our parcels and collected Leonard from the stallkeeper, who'd been guarding him for us. Then, with great difficulty, we pushed our way back through the crowds to the main road and eventually managed to hail a taxi, though the driver scowled at Leonard as if he might have had fleas. And then we had the hysterical problem of trying to drag Flip's new pet up the stairs to his flat! In the end, we sort of lolloped him up, rocking his paws up a stair at a time. By the time we'd arranged all Flip's new purchases, and parked Leonard next to the sofa, we were exhausted.

Flip sank down onto the cushions, with a deep sigh. 'There's some orange juice in the fridge, Zoom. Go and fetch us a couple,' he requested, with a vague wave of his hand. I complied, and even managed to find some ice-cubes to put in it. I sat down next to him, feeling relaxed in his company for the first time.

'Where's your flatmate this weekend?' I asked.

'Oh, I don't know. He said something about taking a boat out on some lake. With a bit of luck, he's drowned himself.'

Just as I was about to ask why he kept Del on as a flatmate if he disliked him so much, the phone went and Flip got up to answer it.

'Huh? . . . No, I didn't remember. I don't think you told me . . . Oh, come on, Jake, it's a nice day. What's wrong with you? . . . Yes, I know we've got the tour coming up, but— Okay, okay, I'll be along at six, if I really have to. Yeah, see you then.'

He replaced the receiver with a bang and looked so angry that I thought he was about to fly off into a tantrum.

'He's a real old woman, is Jake! All he ever thinks about is rehearsals. Honestly, if anyone knows those numbers inside out, it's me. I wrote the damn things, after all! What do I need to practise them for?'

I glanced at my watch. It was just after four. 'Perhaps I'd better go,' I suggested.

'You've no need to rush off yet, there's plenty of time . . .' He put his arm round me and steered me back to the sofa. Then he put his other arm round me, too, and pulled me against his chest. Immediately, I was full of the trembles and quivers I always got when he was near. His lips brushed mine gently once or twice, then settled on my mouth. Our kiss went on and on. I was drowning in it. I no longer knew where I was, or even what day or year it was. There was just Flip and me in the whole universe. There was a golden mist in front of my eyes and I was acutely aware of every tiny bit of my body that was in contact with any part of him.

Then, in a single, graceful movement, he rose to his feet, pulling me with him. 'Come on, Zoom,' he murmured. 'Come on, sweetheart . . .'

He began steering me across the lounge, towards a closed door. I was halfway there before I suddenly stalled, my feet anchoring me to the floor.

'No, Flip – no, I *can't*.' My voice came out all husky and quavery, because I was in a panic. I'd just realised he was pulling me towards his bedroom!

He stopped, and raised one eyebrow. 'No?' he echoed mockingly. 'Oh well. I'd better get off to that rehearsal then.'

He started roaming round the flat, putting his guitar in its case, picking up scraps of paper with song words on, completely ignoring me. I felt awful. I knew I must have really hurt him with my refusal. I'd taken it for granted that, knowing I was still at school, he'd guess I didn't have any experience at . . . well, love, sex, all that sort of thing. So, swallowing hard, I went up to him and touched his arm.

'Flip . . . look, I'm sorry . . .' I fumbled.

He looked up. 'It's okay, baby,' he said briskly.

'Will you . . . I will see you again, won't I?' I hated the beseeching tone that crept into my voice.

Flip looked surprised. Then he grinned. 'Of course. I'm not going to let old Zoom zoom off out of my life, am I? You've got to make some more clothes for me yet.'

'And there's the photo session,' I reminded him.

'Oh yes . . .' He looked a bit absent, and went back to getting his things together.

I made for the door, feeling a lot happier. He hadn't been angry with me. He hadn't finished with me. In fact, he'd been absolutely wonderful about it, just as if he perfectly understood. It was great, the way he'd passed it off so casually, without making the fuss I guessed some blokes would make.

'See you soon,' he promised as I walked out of the door.

Chapter 13

Next day at work, there was a full complement. Joe and Griff were back from their various meetings and travels, Sarah was sitting at the reception desk, looking like an exotic flower in a bright orange blouse and tiny white canvas skirt, Paul gave me a cheery grin as he shouldered past me to get to his office, and Chrissy's voice could be heard hooting with laughter as she chatted to various contacts of hers on the phone.

There were loads of labels to type. They were to go on the envelopes into which all the press information and photographs of Flip and his group were to be put — but, as yet, everyone was to be kept waiting for them until the new set of pictures had been taken. Chrissy had said that the pictures could be got ready in about three days, once they'd been taken, and the fact sheets about the band had already been printed. Joe had brought them in this very morning, after the printers had delivered them, and had stacked them on the floor by my desk. As soon as he'd left, I'd picked one up. There was a potted biography of each member of the group, but I was only interested in one.

'FLIP SAUVAGE. This talented 20-year-old hails

from Portsmouth, where he showed his musical skills at an early age by writing the music for school plays. He appeared at local clubs as a solo singer-songwriter before forming his first group, Solstice, at the age of 16 . . .'

The piece went on, filling in his musical history, mentioning his interests, which included something he described as 'café society'. I made a mental note to ask Chrissy what it meant, then sneakily folded the sheet up small, and popped it into my bag to take home. I felt sure they'd never miss one.

I could hear voices in the corridor outside my office. It was Chrissy talking to Joe.

'Right. I've arranged the photographer for three. Do you think we'll be able to drag him out of his pit by then?'

I wondered who she meant, the photographer, or one of the band. I soon found out.

'I sometimes think that boy's got a built-in resistance to getting rich and famous,' Joe grumbled. 'He's got it all going for him, but he's so damned idle. It's as if he expects the world to come to him. Jake says he didn't bother turning up for rehearsal yesterday morning, and was out most of the afternoon when he tried to call him. That's no behaviour for a band with a record that looks like becoming a hit. What's he going to be like on tour, for God's sake? His attitude's totally wrong.'

Their voices grew fainter, so that I couldn't make out the words any more, and I guessed they'd gone into Joe's office. I felt shocked. I remembered how Flip had been when he'd played those songs to me. He'd been completely carried away – in another world. How could anyone say he didn't care about his music? I knew that it meant more to him than anything. I longed to go out there and stick up for him, but I didn't dare. Anyway, I had something even more pressing on my mind. The photo session tomorrow . . .

Why hadn't Chrissy said anything to me about it? After all, Flip specifically wanted me to be there. I curbed my impatience, telling myself that she'd probably mention it before the end of the day — but, to my horror, halfway through the afternoon I heard her yelling goodbye to Sarah, telling her to take messages if there were any phone calls for her. I just didn't know what to do. Surely Flip couldn't have forgotten to ask her? My ideas were such an important part of the session — *the* most important part, really. He had to look right, otherwise the band just wouldn't make the proper impact on tour or on telly.

I went home in a terrible mood, knowing I'd have to ask Chrissy in the morning. I felt like phoning Flip, yet, at the same time, I didn't want it to seem as if I was pushing myself. After all, who was I? I might have lots of bright ideas, but I was still in school, worse luck.

Karen phoned and wanted to come round, but I was still in a bad temper. When she greeted me with, 'Hi, Belinda,' I snapped at her.

'I refuse to be called Belinda. I've already told you my nickname — *Zoom*. That's what I want you to call me, from now on, so you might as well get practising.'

There was a silence. Then: 'The others didn't think much of you not turning up yesterday . . .'

'I don't care,' I grunted defensively.

'It seems like this bloke really has got a hold on you.

There's no point in asking you to go to the cinema with Ian and me then, is there?'

'Hey, wait a minute . . .' It was too late. She'd put the phone down in a huff. Now I was even more upset and angry. Going to see a film might just have distracted me from Flip and the photo session problem.

I stalked up to my room and tried to take my mind off everything by trying out a few sketches, but inspiration refused to come. Instead, I found myself drawing Flip — frontface, profile, head-and-shoulders portrait, and full length, looking as I wanted him to look on his photos, and on stage. Then I sighed and put down my pencil. Once again, thinking of him had suffused me with heat, as if I were basking in glorious sunshine, just like I'd felt in the café on Sunday. I thought of the way he'd kissed me on the sofa, and the way he'd tried, as if in a trance, to guide me into his bedroom. Perhaps I should have gone with him. Maybe he had nothing more in mind than a prolonged kiss and cuddle, in more comfort than awkwardly scrunched up on the sofa.

On the other hand . . . Familiar, uncomfortable prickles of fear broke out in me. Why was it all so difficult? If I'd had Mum there, I could have asked her what to do under such circumstances, followed her guidance. But, at times like that, you always found yourself alone, and there was no set of rules, no code to follow. I was sure I'd done the right thing in saying no — that's what Mum would have advised. Yet maybe she knew better. Perhaps she'd have told me to trust him, that my suspicions were all in my mind. Yet I felt instinctively that he hadn't just wanted me to go in there to read a book, or hear a tape of his latest songs . . .

Chapter 14

Chrissy sat behind her desk stiffly, scarcely moving, looking as if she was incapable of walking across the carpet, and had been lowered into her chair by a winch. I watched, fascinated, as her arm moved out jerkily, like a robot's, towards her mug of evil-looking black coffee.

'Hangover,' she whispered. 'I'll be all right when I've finished this.'

I'd been on tenterhooks that morning, thinking she wasn't going to turn up but was going to go straight to the photographic session. If she'd done that, I'd have missed my last chance, the one I'd been summoning up all my courage to take.

'It's . . . it's about this afternoon,' I began falteringly. The shadows under her eyes were a most interesting shade of mauve, I noticed; one I'd never seen used as a fabric dye, possibly because it was impossible to reproduce its subtlety. When I was terribly nervous or anxious, I often found myself noticing details like this, as if I'd suddenly become detached from my painful feelings.

Chrissy was blinking owlishly at me, as if she hardly

had the strength to hold her eyelids open. I went on.

'Flip said he wanted me to come along, to advise him on his clothes and things...' My voice jerked to a standstill, and so did my powers of ingenuity. I felt sure she'd think I was lying; that I was nothing but a silly little groupie who'd taken a fancy to Flip on account of his handsome face. She was probably used to fobbing off his fans.

'When did he say this?' she asked, in a croaky whisper.

My mind really was a blank now. What could I say, without giving away the fact that I'd been meeting Flip secretly? 'At the *Top of the Pops* rehearsal,' I improvised feebly.

'Oh, well... that was a few days ago now. He's probably forgotten. He does have a memory like a sieve.' She managed a weak smile. 'I don't know if it'll be all right. I can't give you permission, you'll have to ask Griff. Ouch! My head!' she groaned as the telephone jangled loudly.

I tiptoed out of her office and was just wandering thoughtfully down the corridor when I heard her calling to me. She was hanging onto the doorframe as if she couldn't stand up without it, and in her droopy black skirt and baggy black overblouse, she looked even more witch-like than usual.

She was holding out her mug. 'Be a darling and make me another of the same, could you?' she requested. 'I'll die without it. I honestly don't know why I punish my body like this. I suppose I must have thought it was fun at the time.'

She paused as if to catch her breath, and I made a

mental note never ever to start going to pubs if it made you feel as bad as this.

'That was yet another bloody journalist asking for up-to-date photographs of Flip,' she told me. 'I don't know about doing the whole works on him – any old holiday snaps would do at the moment. But if I don't get something soon, we'll lose all the impetus created by that television appearance.'

As I stood in the cubbyhole under the stairs, waiting for the kettle to boil, I thought about what she'd said and felt quite upset and indignant. Of *course* getting the right sort of publicity pictures mattered! Even Griff had said at my interview that having the right image mattered to anyone, not just pop stars. Why wasn't he insisting on doing things right? It was as if everyone except Flip and me was suddenly devoid of ideas and vision.

My father still had some copies of an old magazine about the Beatles, and he'd told me about how everyone went mad about their daringly long hairstyles when they first started getting famous. He'd got into awful trouble from his mum for insisting on doing the same. Then there were people like Boy George, with his outrageous make-up and women's clothes. No-one could ignore things like that. It was part and parcel of a group or singer's act.

I sighed as I splashed boiling water into the line of mugs in front of me. When I took Griff his, he asked me to sit down.

'There's something I need to talk to you about,' he said. With a jolt of excitement, I wondered if he, or someone else – maybe the guy at the BBC who'd asked for my number – wanted me to design them something. But my hopeful thoughts were dashed when he announced: 'I've heard from Sandy. She's fine now, and the doctors have signed her off. She's bored stiff at home and she wants to come back to work as soon as possible – the end of next week, to be precise. She'd like to ease herself back into it by doing next Thursday and Friday, then start back properly the week after – that's a week next Monday.'

The blood was thundering in my ears and I had to strain to hear him. He couldn't mean it! I thought frantically. Not when I was enjoying myself so much. Not when there were so many opportunities opening up for me. And this place was my main link with Flip! How would I ever find out what was happening to him on tour if I wasn't here? Griff was still talking.

'How have you been finding things here? I'm sorry I haven't had a proper chat with you before now, but what with going to France and everything...' He grinned apologetically, but his smile faded when he noticed the expression on my face. 'Don't look so miserable, lovey. What is it? Is it the money? Perhaps I can pay you a bit extra, as compensation, sort of.'

He was being so kind. 'No, it's not the money,' I assured him. 'It's... nothing really. It's just been fun, that's all.' I gave a little shrug and tried to cheer up. 'I'll be able to catch up on my studies. I'll be getting my O-level results any day now.'

'I hope you do well,' Griff said brightly. 'I bet you've got... let me see... ah yes, Pisces rising. That would explain your artistic streak and your moods. I can tell you're one of those people who's either right up, or right down. Now—'

'But I told you at my interview that I was a Libra, so what's all this Pisces rising business?' I enquired, perplexed.

He started explaining the basics of astrology, but it was far too complicated for me. Anyway, time was ticking on. It was nearly lunchtime, and Chrissy would soon be leaving. Griff seemed in a chatty, friendly mood, so I plucked up all my courage. It didn't really matter what he thought of me any more, anyway, as I'd be leaving a week on Wednesday . . . a week *tomorrow*! I could hardly believe it. I couldn't bear it.

I butted in desperately, just when he was in the middle of trying to explain what squares and oppositions were all about. 'Griff . . . there's something I've got to ask you about.'

He ran his fingers through his fair, fuzzy curls and looked faintly surprised.

'Please can I go to the photo session with Chrissy this afternoon? When I made Flip that shirt, he said he thought I had some good ideas about style and image, and I might be able to help him and the band with theirs. I'd love to help if I can, but only if you can spare me, of course,' I added hastily.

'That young man needs more than a change of image to get him to the top. What he could do with is half a ton of application. I think Joe's picked a loser there. It's a pity, because, with the boy's looks . . .'

He didn't finish his sentence, just left the implication hanging in the air. My jaw muscles clenched in anger. Why were people always moaning about Flip? It struck me that perhaps I was the only person to know the real

Flip Sauvage; not his manager, not his PR lady, maybe not even his group, but just me. I wished I could think of something to say to stick up for him, but I couldn't.

'You'd better ask Sarah,' he said absently, already flipping through some papers on his desk, as if I wasn't there. 'If she's got no work for you, then it's okay by me.'

I babbled my thanks and went off to ask Sarah. I wasn't looking forward to it because she seemed in a pretty bad mood, and her reply confirmed my worst fears.

'Sorry, you can't go anywhere, I'm afraid.' Her voice was cold and unfriendly which just added to how devastatingly upset I felt. 'I've got to go to the dentist's so you'll have to look after the switchboard this afternoon.'

The switchboard! I felt like uprooting it from its cables and smashing it onto the floor. I belted into my office, closed the door, and sank my head onto the typewriter and dripped tears into its dusty interior. It was so unfair. I could have done so much for Flip's future. When *was* I going to see him again?

'That's bad luck, dear,' Dad sympathised that night, when I told my parents about the job. 'Never mind. At least you've got four weeks' money. That's more than some of your friends will have. And it's been good experience, too. Are they quite within their rights, though, to take somebody on for a specified period and then ask them to leave before that time?'

'I'm sure they'd have given me the push before now if I hadn't fitted in, or hadn't worked well,' I pointed out, hunching myself glumly into my favourite seat in the lounge, the old, squashy armchair by the fireplace. Not that it was a real fireplace any more. Mum and Dad had fitted a gas fire instead, which I thought was a shame because, when I was little, I used to love gazing into the flames.

'Still, perhaps I ought to give them a ring,' Dad was musing.

I shot bolt upright in my chair. 'No, don't do that. I don't want you interfering,' I shot at him.

Mum gave me a sharp look. 'Don't talk like that to your father, dear, he was only trying to help,' she warned.

'No-one can help,' I grunted glumly. 'Oh, just as things were going so well too . . . I mean, someone might have offered me a real job designing costumes or something. That man at the BBC studios was really interested. If *only* I'd given him my number.'

Dad muttered something to Mum which I didn't quite catch, then said: 'You wait until you get your exam results before you start talking about getting jobs. We're not having you throw away an education just to get mixed up with some pop group.'

'Why not? *You* nearly did,' I replied accusingly.

'That was different,' he rapped sternly. 'I wasn't one of the brightest people in my class, like you are. I left school at sixteen because I had to.'

'Well, maybe I'll have to, as well,' I snarled. I was in a really prickly mood. They were both getting on my nerves. Why couldn't they just leave me alone and watch telly?

'Don't talk like that, Belinda!' Mum commanded. 'We both hope you'll do well, but even if you don't, it's not the end of the world. You can always sit one of the subjects again. You should be getting the results any day now, shouldn't you? They might even be here tomorrow.'

'Oh Mum – don't!' I yelled, covering up my ears. 'I don't want to talk about it. I don't even want to *think* about it!'

But my O-level results weren't the most important thing to think about, though they were bad enough. What I needed was the answer to the questions that were making me so jumpy and grouchy and touchy; was I Flip's girlfriend, or was he just playing with me? How often did normal boyfriends contact their girlfriends and take them out? How long would I have to wait? When I left G.R. next week, would he even hear about it? And would he instantly forget me once I'd gone? Why hadn't he mentioned the photographic session again? Was it because I'd been too cheeky and pushy and he'd only said I could come in order to humour me?

I fell asleep that night with all this churning round my brain, but the next morning the *other* dreaded subject reared its ugly head, in the shape of a long, white envelope . . .

Chapter 15

'Never mind,' Mum said consolingly, patting my shoulder. 'You've done well at Art, and you never thought you'd get such a high mark for Geography, did you?'

'But I've failed History!' I wailed. 'Oh, Mum . . .that was going to be one of my three A-level subjects. I don't know what I'm going to do now.'

Dad came in and said Jen was on the phone. 'I don't want to talk to her – tell her I'll call her back,' I yelled hoarsely, through my tears. 'Tell her I'm in the bath or something. Don't tell her I've read my results yet, or she'll get suspicious.'

He went off, and seconds later the phone went again. This time it was Karen. 'Tell her the post came after I went out to work,' I ordered.

We were all late for work that morning, Mum, Dad and me.

'I can't go in like this,' I gulped. 'Just look at me.'

'Splash your face with cold water and put some of my moisturiser on it,' Mum suggested sensibly. 'Now, I really must be going. We can talk all this over tonight. It's not the end of the world, you know. Perhaps it's fate's way of telling you it was a rotten idea to try doing A-level History, anyway.'

'Thanks, Mum,' I said, grateful for her attempt to cheer me up.

'I still think it's worth going out to celebrate the results. What's one failure? You've passed six, and I'm proud of you, Belinda. We both are,' Dad assured me, grinning all over his face. 'Just think of all the poor people who haven't passed anything!'

'I'd rather not. Some of my friends might be amongst them,' I commented gloomily.

After all my tears, I developed a raging headache. It was decided that I wouldn't go in, even though it would mean losing some pay. I promised to try and get there after lunch, and Mum said she'd ring Griff and tell him I wasn't well. Then they both went off and left me to wallow.

History . . . I'd tried so hard to memorise all the dates of the battles, the places where they were fought, the names and years of rule of the various kings and queens, the treaties, the religious phases. I loved History. I couldn't understand how I could have failed. There had to be some mistake. It would be truly terrible if I couldn't take it for A-level. There wasn't another subject I could even remotely imagine taking.

I sat morosely at the kitchen table, thinking of how I'd miss reading about the lifestyles of people from ages past; what they wore, how their homes were furnished, what their buildings looked like. History had always been such a source of inspiration to me. It was worth having to swot up on all the tedious things, the battles and the political treaties, to get to the parts that really interested me. The trouble was that our History lessons had been mostly about the boring stuff and not nearly enough about what interested me.

That thought hit me like a great revelation. What I liked wasn't the History you needed to pass exams with; that part was what I'd always found difficult and dull. Suddenly, a great weight lifted off my back, as if I'd just removed a heavy rucksack. If I didn't take History, I wouldn't have to sweat over memorising all the tedious bits! I'd enjoy the subject far more if I was free to read about the way-of-life side of things, instead of wars, which I hated. I never could bear bloodshed and have never understood why statesmen found it necessary to risk the lives of millions of innocent people.

I gave a shudder, and reached once more for the list of results, which I'd crammed back into the envelope out of sight. Art, English and History; that was what I'd intended to take. But why shouldn't it be Art, English and Geography? The only reason why I hadn't planned to take A-level Geography was because Art was my best subject at school, English my second best, and History something I really enjoyed – or thought I did. But, come to think of it, I'd been getting quite good marks for Geography during the last three or four terms. And I liked it because it was a subject you could see. You could actually walk through a glaciated valley and look at it and understand it, whereas History was . . . ghosts, and faded ink on paper treaties.

The headache pill I'd taken half an hour earlier was beginning to work. I thought of going in to the office, then thought, why waste the morning? Mum's told them I won't be there until at least lunchtime. A little, wicked thrill shivered through me at the thought of having four stolen hours to play with. I could go round and see Karen, perhaps, or call on one of my other friends I hadn't seen for ages. Or – and the extreme sinfulness of this idea made me blink at my own audacity – I could take the tube to Sloane Square. I didn't have to ring his bell or anything. I could just walk down the Kings Road, window-shopping, then saunter slowly down his street and just see if there were any signs of life on the third floor of his house . . .

The temptation was too great to ignore. I flew upstairs, flung on a dress I'd made out of some highly unusual material with what I thought was a medieval-looking pattern on, and set out for the tube.

I got there so fast that I felt almost as if I'd been teleported there, like they do in science fiction films. In no time at all, it seemed, I was at the end of Flip's road and seconds later I was outside his house. There was a large blue van parked outside. Nosily, I peeped through the back window and spotted two large, round black cases which could have been for drums.

My pulse-rate quickened. Perhaps one or more of the band were visiting Flip, talking about the tour or something. I knew I couldn't hang about for long, but I was reluctant to leave, knowing that Flip was up there. Talk about being so near, yet so far! Just a few flights of stairs separated me from his wonderful face, his tender, sensitive touch, his spellbinding music, his kisses . . .

I leant against the railings and, from time to time, glanced both ways down the road and consulted my watch, to make any observer think I was waiting for someone. I didn't want some interfering neighbour to ring the police and tell them there was a loiterer lurking around!

After I'd been there about twenty minutes and was just persuading myself that I'd better move on, the front door burst open and Stu, Rod and Jake came out. But Flip wasn't with them. They sounded as if they'd been arguing because their voices were loud and abrupt, and they slammed the door behind them with a crash that echoed right down the street.

Then they saw me. 'Oh, hello. What are you doing here? No work today?' Jake enquired. He sounded embarrassed, probably because he'd just uttered a few swear words and realised I must have heard.

It would have sounded silly to say I was just passing, so I decided to tell the truth. 'I was coming to see Flip. About some costume ideas I'd had.'

'So he didn't tell you, either?' Jake narrowed his eyes and looked at me suspiciously. 'Are you sure you don't know anything about it?'

'About what?' I asked in consternation. 'What's happened?'

'That's what we'd all like to know,' Rod said sneeringly.

'Are you going into town?' Jake asked, and when I nodded, he invited: 'Jump in, then, Zoom. We'll give you a lift.'

Stu and Rod obligingly climbed into the back and sat on the floor, and I got in beside Jake, who was driving. He set off in silence, but the other two were muttering in the back, and I could make out the odd word. They seemed to be talking about summer holidays abroad – someone else's, by the sound of it. The name Marbella cropped up a few times, and some girl's name was mentioned. I wasn't paying much attention.

'Don't tell anyone you've seen me this morning,' I begged Jake. 'It's true that I didn't feel well earlier. But then I got a bit better and decided to look at a few shops and go into work this afternoon.'

Jake gave me a look that was full of a sympathy and understanding that was beyond my comprehension. 'So he's let you down too, girl,' he said.

'Pardon?' I didn't have a clue what he was on about.

'Flip. I know you've been seeing him. He told me,' he replied. I felt quite flattered that he'd considered his relationship with me important enough to talk about. But my pleasure was to be short-lived.

'None of us can understand him,' Jake continued. 'The record's doing well, we've got an album and a tour lined up, and he has to go and do this. You can imagine how we feel. Without him, we're nothing. Right on the brink of stardom, due to start earning some real money for the first time in our lives, and now it'll be back to square one, joining some unknown band, filling in with session work, waiting to get discovered all over again. We're going to try suing him – not that we think we'll get anywhere, but that's how bitter we all feel.'

'Yeah. Too right,' put in a voice from behind me.

All the time Jake had been talking, I could feel the joy and energy draining out of me, leaving nothing but dread and fear. I was cold – so cold my hands felt like ice, even though it was a humid August day. 'What's happened? Has the band split up?' I asked in a cracked voice.

'Seems like it,' Jake scoffed. 'What else are we to think when our star attraction vanishes to a villa in Marbella, on the whim of some rich bird who owns it? We came round this morning to pick him up and take him to the rehearsal, which was our only way of making sure he'd be there, because he's let us down so often, and what do we get? His stupid mate Del with some garbled message about how this bird dragged him off to the airport at the crack of dawn.

'He didn't tell any of us he was thinking of taking a holiday. He didn't even mention it to Joe. You should have heard what *he* said when we rang him up just now and told him! Not that Joe would have let him take a holiday now. We've got too much lined up – well, we did have . . .'

My mind was racing over the facts. Some girl dragged him off very early this morning . . . that meant she must have spent the *night* with him! My stomach gave a kind of lurch at the thought and I could feel the muscles in it contracting, as if I'd been kicked, or had all the breath knocked out of me. Oh, Flip . . . I yearned silently, closing my eyes. Why did you do this to me?

Chapter 16

Very little work was done by anybody that afternoon. All they could do was discuss Flip, and the significance of what he'd done. One of the first things I overheard was a shouting match between Griff and Joe.

'I told you not to trust that boy!' Griff hurled. 'I knew all along that he was bad news. If you'd just believed me, think of all the time and money we could have saved! What about that advance you insisted on paying him? I suggest you get it back – and fast! He was our biggest potential breadwinner, that boy—'

'I know, you don't have to ram it down my throat,' Joe shouted aggressively back. 'What do you think I am? Bloody psychic? I'll admit the boy had a few problems—'

'You call being born without any sense of responsibility whatsoever a *problem*?' Griff snapped back. 'I call it a flaming disability!'

'Well, you and your useless astrology – why didn't you see it coming in the stars, so we could have got our cash out in time? As it is, we've booked the studios, we'll have to pay them a compensation fee, we've got the photographer to pay, the printers, to say nothing of trying to pacify the band. And what do we tell the press?'

'Ask Chrissy. She'll think of something. Zoom? Get me Phil, the accountant!' Joe screeched his order and I wondered unhappily, not for the first time since I'd got in, why it was my luck to have to look after the switchboard. Apparently Sarah had had a tooth out the previous day, which probably explained her bad mood beforehand, as she either had toothache or was scared stiff. She hadn't come in today as she was still feeling groggy so, with me absent too, the morning had been chaos.

I had little time to mope about Flip because, for the rest of the day, I had orders barked at me to get this person, then that, book calls to the States and Europe, ring certain continental hotels and cancel reservations, then make a note to tell Sarah to type out confirming letters . . . it was pure panic. And all the time I was conscious of the fact that the creator of this bedlam was sunning himself on a beach somewhere with some stunning, sophisticated girl. If only that girl could have been me . . .

I thought back to the fantasy I'd had about photographers snapping us at the airport: 'Flip Sauvage and his mystery girl, whom the world knows only as Zoom.' Flip and Zoom . . . Now I'd probably open the paper tomorrow morning and see him pictured with this other mystery girl. A stab of pure jealousy made me wince. How *could* he do this to me?

'I feel sorry for that group of his,' Dad sympathised when I told my parents about it. 'Having been in a group myself, I know just how they must be feeling.'

If only somebody knew how *I* must be feeling, I thought bitterly. I hadn't told Mum and Dad anything about my feelings towards Flip, but somehow Mum must have guessed. She waited till Dad had gone out of the room for something, put her arm round me and gave me a comforting squeeze, and said: 'You were rather keen on him, weren't you, love?'

It wasn't just my face and neck that blushed this time; I felt as if I were on fire all over, with shame and embarrassment. Had my feelings really been that transparent? How could I have been such a bad judge of a character and a situation? How could I have let myself get so easily taken in and misled?

Mum didn't expect an answer. 'Don't worry, it'll pass,' was all she said, and I was grateful for that. I didn't want a great, deep, searching heart-to-heart about boys and love affairs. I wasn't ready for all that. Anyway, this hadn't been a real relationship, a boyfriend-girlfriend thing. A mere two measly dates; what could you call that? And he hadn't exactly taken me out anywhere, either. But he had kissed me – how could I ever forget that? And his singing . . . I knew it would haunt me for ever, like his grey eyes would, and his cheekbones and chiselled profile, and his hair, like yellow satin.

I couldn't get out of phoning Karen. She, to her utter horror, had failed Maths, so we both had something to commiserate about, especially her, as she loathed Maths anyway. Now she'd have to re-sit it, as it was one of the subjects she needed in order to work towards her Zoology degree.

'Come round,' she begged. 'Ian's mate Tony's brought one of those big wine-box things full of cider.'

Even the thought of cider, and Ian, couldn't persuade me to be sociable. I didn't feel like telling her about what had happened with Flip, and she'd be bound to ask whether or not I'd seen him. She filled me in on the exam results of some of our classmates. Jen had passed four, Gordon Monks, who lived in Karen's road, had only passed one, Kim had got five. But it was Bev who'd surprised us all by doing spectacularly well for someone who intended to leave and become a child bride! She'd passed all eight she'd taken, with really high grades, too. It really would be a terrible waste if she threw it all away and got married, I thought.

'Look, I haven't felt very well today,' I explained. Well, it was half true. 'I'll see you tomorrow night, I promise. Then, after next Wednesday, I'll be seeing loads more of you because my job's ending.'

'Oh . . . bad luck,' she said, sounding quite sincere, and I forgave her her offishness when we last met.

Friday passed in a flash. Nobody would listen to Chrissy when she suggested that Flip's disappearing act could be sold to the press as a real one: 'Pop Star Vanishes On Eve Of Tour'. I was glad I was leaving the following week. Hearing Flip's name on everyone's lips, eight hours a day, was too much for me. It was sheer torture. With every mention of him, I was reminded of my foolish fantasies about him. I'd seen Dad's point and I now felt very sorry for Jake and the others. They were all serious musicians, willing to work hard for a chance of stardom. But Flip expected it all to come to him without him having to lift a finger.

I thought of him that day in the shop, parading and posing in the clothes he was trying on, before the appreciative audience of the salesgirls and me. Then I remembered how he'd gone mad over the stuffed animals in the market. I'd thought it fun then, and that it showed what an uninhibited sense of humour he had. But now I could see that even this was for effect. He was nothing but an insincere poser. He dabbled with this and that, with fashion, antiques, the music business, but never dedicated himself to anything. All he cared about was himself and what other people thought about him. He used people. Why, he'd never even paid me for the shirt I'd made, I remembered unhappily.

Yet those songs . . . he did have talent. It was such a shame that, as Griff so rightly observed, he lacked the application to get anywhere. I could see him drifitng into marriage with some rich, beautiful, empty-headed society girl, and doing nothing but jet-setting around the world for the rest of his life, being seen in the most fashionable places. I loathed him. I was glad I'd had such a lucky escape. I knew it would take me a long time to forget his kisses, and even longer to forget his haunting face, if I was going to keep finding it in newspapers and magazines. But I was glad – so, so glad – that I'd done nothing to feel bad or guilty about. Nothing at all . . .

On Saturday morning, an invitation to Bev and Simon's wedding arrived. I went to Karen's – she'd had one, too – and we sat in her back room watching the dismal spectacle of rain sluicing down the windows and flooding the flowerbeds.

'Look,' Karen exclaimed, thrusting my invitation under my nose. 'It says you can take someone. I've already invited Terry Cartmel – you know, the tall one from 5B who's in the football team. I was lucky – bumped into him in the library and just asked him on the spur of the moment, and he said yes. Isn't it great? What a pity you can't bring Flip Whatsisname.'

'Don't remind me,' I said sourly. 'I don't mind going on my own.'

'You can take our Ian if you like,' she suggested slyly. 'He won't be doing anything a fortnight on Saturday . . .'

For some reason, my face began to tingle as I asked: 'Why?'

'She's given him the push!' Karen let out a hearty bellow of laughter.

'Sssh!' I went. 'How do you know he's not sobbing his heart out in his room? If he hears you laughing at him, he might take it into his head to jump out of the window!' I wasn't serious, of course.

'No, he's gone down to the record shop with his mates. Then they said something about going swimming,' she informed me.

'Swimming? In this weather?' I screwed my face up in dismay.

'Well, no-one else will be there. The baths will be empty,' Karen pointed out sensibly.

It suddenly seemed like the best idea in the world to go up to the baths and join them, so I dashed home for my things.

Karen had been right. There was hardly anyone in the pool. We'd been sitting on the edge, swinging our legs and trying to persuade each other to go in first, for about ten minutes before they all trooped in. Ian looked surprised to see me.

'Belinda!' he cried. 'Sorry, I mean Zoom!'

'It's Belinda again now,' I informed him glumly. 'You can forget all that Zoom business.' Even Bin-bag would be quite nice, I thought nostalgically. What was all this 'Belinda' business?

'Oh, I forgot. You've, er . . . been going through a bit of what I've been going through, haven't you? Karen told me.' He smiled sympathetically. I squinted up at him. He was wearing a pair of brief blue trunks and he was quite tanned. For the first time ever, I thought what a nice body he had; well-shaped legs, flat stomach, muscular shoulders . . .

Stop it! I told myself sternly. You've known Ian all these years. You can't start thinking things like that about him now!

Suddenly, ice-cold water was smacking me in the face and I was screaming: 'You beast!' at Ian, who'd pushed me in. Then Karen grabbed him and ducked him, and we got told off by the attendant for larking around.

As I struck out through the blue water, I experienced a sense of worry-free freedom that I hadn't known for ages. It was as if someone had wiped the slate clean and enabled me to start again. I only had things to look forward to. I had no regrets. I'd just gone completely off boys with blond hair.

Chapter 17

Everone was terribly sweet to me on my last day at work. They took me out to an Italian restaurant and we all had spaghetti and red wine and the afternoon was a blur after that. On the tube journey home, however, I felt horribly flat. I'd learned so much in four weeks. My typing was better, I knew how to operate a switchboard – and I'd really enjoyed making phone calls abroad, booking plane tickets, organising hotels and even tidying up the filing system. The thought of having to go back to sitting in a classroom and swotting for exams, when the rest of the world was doing real things in offices, was quite appalling.

'Mum,' I complained when I got home, 'why couldn't I leave now and get a job? There's so much I could do in an office. It's so much fun . . .'

Mum shook her head. 'You were in an exceptional place if you think all offices are fun,' she said. 'Mine's deadly boring, all those old fogeys of solicitors and those filing cabinets that you're not allowed to touch in case you displace some useless document that's been sitting there since 1924.

'And anyway,' she went on, 'you mightn't find it so easy to get a job. You were lucky to get this one. The music business is a very specialised industry. There's an awful lot of competition to get in. You'd probably end up as an ordinary filing clerk in a ghastly, dead-as-doornails insurance company or something. At least, if you go to college, you'll have spent a few years protected from all that, enjoying yourself, and bringing out the talent that you've got.'

She gripped my hand. 'Your dad and I are very proud of you, Belinda,' she told me firmly. 'You've obviously gained an awful lot from this job, and it was wonderful seeing that boy wearing your shirt on television. I only wished we'd had a video so we could have recorded it and kept it.'

'Belinda Harker's first successful design was a Renaissance-inspired overshirt, modelled on *Top of the Pops* by Flip Sauvage, cult figure of the Eighties,' I intoned, trying to sound like the voice-over on a TV documentary.

We both chuckled. Mum withdrew her hand and leaned back in her chair. 'Is that what you'd really like to be, dear?' she asked. 'A fashion designer?'

I nodded eagerly. 'And someday I'd like to own my own chain of shops, just selling my clothes. And perhaps we'll offer a sort of package deal to famous personalities, doing their make-up and hair and developing a personal style for them. I'd really love that,' I sighed.

There was an expression of fond amusement on Mum's face. 'You can start with your dad if you like,' she offered, with a wry grin. 'I went through his wardrobe this afternoon and he's got some shirts in there which he's had all the time I've known him, and he won't throw them away.'

'Perhaps I ought to bring that back, then,' I suggested, chortling with mirth. 'The Sixties Man — a throw-back to when flower power meant more than sticking manure on your roses!'

We both shrieked. Then Dad came in, so we had to shut up, quick.

'Those office skills you've learned will come in useful if you ever do start your own business one day,' Mum pointed out, and I agreed.

I found myself wondering what everyone else from school had done in the holidays. Suddenly, I was dying to get back there, just so I could tell them about what had happened to me. Would they believe me? I didn't really care. I knew it was true, even if it was already feeling like a dream I'd just woken up from. Did I really make that shirt for Flip? Did he really kiss me? Perhaps I'd go out and buy his single, as a kind of souvenir.

My fingers were itching to make something. Bev's wedding was coming up. I could design myself something special for that. Something in a bright colour, so that it wouldn't compete with the bride's white wedding gown. Bev had described her outfit in minute detail; Edwardian-inspired, with tight sleeves and lots of foamy lace.

I'd have deep ruby red, something a bit more figure-fitting than my normal loose tunics. After all, I was going with Ian . . .

The thought hit me like a shock-wave. I hadn't actually asked him yet, but Karen said she'd mentioned it to him and he was really keen. My mind went back to the old days, when we used to joke around and tease each other, before his girlfriend had come on the scene. I'd always been fond of him. It was his dreadful clothes that had put me off. Flip had always looked so fabulous . . . But he wasn't a nice person, I reminded myself. And Ian was. So perhaps I'd be able to overlook his slightly old-fashioned trousers, and the shirt that didn't quite go with them.

That day at the baths, though, he'd been looking really tasty. I'd refused to let myself linger on the memory of how he'd looked in his swimming trunks. But afterwards, when we'd dressed and gone for coffee, he'd been wearing lovely, pale cream jeans and a yellow sports top which made his tan look even darker.

He'd asked me how it felt to be out of work, and if it would mean I'd be coming round to their house more often. When I'd said, 'Probably,' he'd replied, 'Good.'

It was strange how people could turn out to be not a bit like you thought they were. Even I'd changed. I was no longer Zoom, designer to the music biz. That had just been a passing phase, like a fashion itself. Now I was Belinda again, but not the old Belinda, who hated her name and had little confidence in herself. Now I'd seen how opportunities could occur, and how you could lose everything if you were careless and unconscientious. Who would ever trust Flip enough to give him a recording contract and money in advance again?

Flip and Belinda would never have worked. It had had to be Flip and Zoom, a beautiful image, brittle, false as the gold paper on a chocolate coin. Now it had all melted away, leaving nothing worthwhile behind. When I tried to draw him now, my pencil wavered on the page. I could no longer quite capture his face.

Ian and Zoom would never work, either. It had to be Ian and Belinda. Funny how he'd been the first to notice that I was no longer Bin-bag but had grown up and become a person in my own right, a girl who was more than just his sister's friend.

I reached for my sketchpad again and drew Ian — and suddenly the ideas began to flow and I rapidly covered sheet after sheet. Then afterwards, I spread the pages out and stared at Ian sporting a variety of different garments; Ian with a beard; Ian with his hair cut and highlighted. And I reached a decision, and piled the pages neatly to one side.

No, I must never try to change Ian. That would be wrong. I could make suggestions perhaps, or give guidance if I was asked for it, but that was all. For it was looking very much as if, at long last, Ian had some pretty good ideas of his own . . .

Fiction

☐	**The Chains of Fate**	Pamela Belle	£2.95p
☐	**Options**	Freda Bright	£1.50p
☐	**The Thirty-nine Steps**	John Buchan	£1.50p
☐	**Secret of Blackoaks**	Ashley Carter	£1.50p
☐	**Hercule Poirot's Christmas**	Agatha Christie	£1.50p
☐	**Dupe**	Liza Cody	£1.25p
☐	**Lovers and Gamblers**	Jackie Collins	£2.50p
☐	**Sphinx**	Robin Cook	£1.25p
☐	**My Cousin Rachel**	Daphne du Maurier	£1.95p
☐	**Flashman and the Redskins**	George Macdonald Fraser	£1.95p
☐	**The Moneychangers**	Arthur Hailey	£2.50p
☐	**Secrets**	Unity Hall	£1.75p
☐	**Black Sheep**	Georgette Heyer	£1.75p
☐	**The Eagle Has Landed**	Jack Higgins	£1.95p
☐	**Sins of the Fathers**	Susan Howatch	£3.50p
☐	**Smiley's People**	John le Carré	£1.95p
☐	**To Kill a Mockingbird**	Harper Lee	£1.95p
☐	**Ghosts**	Ed McBain	£1.75p
☐	**The Silent People**	Walter Macken	£1.95p
☐	**Gone with the Wind**	Margaret Mitchell	£3.50p
☐	**Blood Oath**	David Morrell	£1.75p
☐	**The Night of Morningstar**	Peter O'Donnell	£1.75p
☐	**Wilt**	Tom Sharpe	£1.75p
☐	**Rage of Angels**	Sidney Sheldon	£1.95p
☐	**The Unborn**	David Shobin	£1.50p
☐	**A Town Like Alice**	Nevile Shute	£1.75p
☐	**Gorky Park**	Martin Cruz Smith	£1.95p
☐	**A Falcon Flies**	Wilbur Smith	£2.50p
☐	**The Grapes of Wrath**	John Steinbeck	£2.50p
☐	**The Deep Well at Noon**	Jessica Stirling	£2.50p
☐	**The Ironmaster**	Jean Stubbs	£1.75p
☐	**The Music Makers**	E. V. Thompson	£1.95p

Non-fiction

☐	**The First Christian**	Karen Armstrong	£2.50p
☐	**Pregnancy**	Gordon Bourne	£3.50p
☐	**The Law is an Ass**	Gyles Brandreth	£1.75p
☐	**The 35mm Photographer's Handbook**	Julian Calder and John Garrett	£5.95p
☐	**London at its Best**	Hunter Davies	£2.95p
☐	**Back from the Brink**	Michael Edwardes	£2.95p

☐	**Travellers' Britain**	Arthur Eperon	£2.95p
☐	**Travellers' Italy**		£2.95p
☐	**The Complete Calorie Counter**	Eileen Fowler	80p
☐	**The Diary of Anne Frank**	Anne Frank	£1.75p
☐	**And the Walls Came Tumbling Down**	Jack Fishman	£1.95p
☐	**Linda Goodman's Sun Signs**	Linda Goodman	£2.50p
☐	**Scott and Amundsen**	Roland Huntford	£3.95p
☐	**Victoria RI**	Elizabeth Longford	£4.95p
☐	**Symptoms**	Sigmund Stephen Miller	£2.50p
☐	**Book of Worries**	Robert Morley	£1.50p
☐	**Airport International**	Brian Moynahan	£1.75p
☐	**Pan Book of Card Games**	Hubert Phillips	£1.95p
☐	**Keep Taking the Tabloids**	Fritz Spiegl	£1.75p
☐	**An Unfinished History of the World**	Hugh Thomas	£3.95p
☐	**The Baby and Child Book**	Penny and Andrew Stanway	£4.95p
☐	**The Third Wave**	Alvin Toffler	£2.95p
☐	**Pauper's Paris**	Miles Turner	£2.50p
☐	**The Psychic Detectives**	Colin Wilson	£2.50p
☐	**The Flier's Handbook**		£5.95p

All these books are available at your local bookshop or newsagent, or can be ordered direct from the publisher. Indicate the number of copies required and fill in the form below

....

Name..
(Block letters please)

Address..

Send to CS Department, Pan Books Ltd, PO Box 40, Basingstoke, Hants
Please enclose remittance to the value of the cover price plus:
35p for the first book plus 15p per copy for each additional book ordered to a maximum charge of £1.25 to cover postage and packing
Applicable only in the UK

While every effort is made to keep prices low, it is sometimes necessary to increase prices at short notice. Pan Books reserve the right to show on covers and charge new retail prices which may differ from those advertised in the text or elsewhere